Fiction, all fantasy, a tale about how our pets might handle an Apocalypse.

By author Thomas M Cook
Copyright - Library of Congress
ISBN: 978-1-9768-8610-2

Comments: https://apocalypticcats.blogspot.com/

For Ainsley, a happy 16th birthday present. (sorry it's late, I don't do deadlines). Your disabilities have, at times, made life difficult. Your cats have always been there for you.

Thanks to my sister Joan for taking the time to proof read this story.

The Apocalyptic House Cats

Chapter 1

Strange. For some time now the cats had noticed that the behaviour of their people had changed. They were people so they were always strange, but that strangeness had increased significantly over the last few months. Now they were gone, the people, and it was not understood why. Or where they had gone. Or when they would be back.

The humans had been doing odd and uncharacteristic things for quite some time. Stocking the cabinets with more food than usual. Turning lights off earlier and keeping a watch out the windows. Seeming to be on edge all the time.

And now they were gone. Taken in the middle of the night by armed and dangerous looking men. It wasn't only their people, the neighbors had been disappearing for weeks. Some loaded up their cars and drove off, to where the cats wondered?

As time wore on more and more people left, the ones who stayed grew more and more tense. Soon there were only a few and now they were gone, forced to leave. As to why this was happening, the cats had no clue.

Now the cats found themselves alone. The first thing they noticed, long before venturing out from their hiding places, was the silence. With people there was always something. Even at night there would be the hum of some nearby electronic device or the rumbling of some distant vehicle. Never this quiet.

Ava, a tiger kitty, brown, black, gray, with big green eyes, peered out first. She had always been much less cautious than the other cat, Sasha. She stuck her head out from behind the sofa, which was her favorite hiding spot, sniffed the fresh morning air, and quickly looked around the room. Seeing nothing alarming she took a few steps forward and crouched back down, looking and listening.

The morning was just beginning to break. It was still very early, the only difference from night being a slight glow in the east announcing the eminent arrival of the sun. It was a crisp morning. The kind of temperature that made a good deep breath feel refreshing, but not so cool as to make one uncomfortably chilly. Especially if you were wearing a nice fur coat.

It was early autumn in Michigan. The last few days had been sunny and warm and it felt like that would continue today. These were the kind of days that might only be distinguished from summer by the numbers on the calendar and the depth of the morning chill. It was early autumn in Michigan and today would be very nearly beach weather, but this being Michigan, it could snow tomorrow.

Ava had always been an indoor cat, she was unconcerned with weather patterns. The time of year only affected her view as she gazed out the window from a comfortable perch on the back of her favorite chair. Sasha spent the first year of her life outside and knew how it felt to be cold, wet, hungry and tired. These were not fond memories. Even though she was an indoor kitty now, she still feared the coming of winter and the cold that came with it. In Michigan that cold could be very dangerous. None of those thoughts ever troubled Ava.

Sasha, with long cream colored hair and black face/ears/feet/tail and the most beautiful blue eyes you've ever seen, noticed Ava moving and decided to leave her hiding place. She had watched the scary events of the night before from under a chair and hadn't moved since. She cautiously crept forward, belly low to the ground, as if at any moment some unknown evil would jump from the shadows and snatch her up.

Nothing happened, no scary creatures seemed to be present, so she joined Ava at the front door. This was the source of the crisp, fresh morning air. The small entryway rug had been dragged across the threshold, during the disturbing nights' events, blocking the door slightly open. Sasha had watched this from under her chair.

The bigger of her humans was the last to be taken. With one foot he had pulled the rug partly out the door as he was forced out of the house. He'd met her eyes at the last possible moment and had given her a small smile and a slight little wink as if to say 'don't worry little girl, it will all be okay'. He always made her feel that way, like everything would be okay. And now he was gone. Sasha thought maybe he'd propped open the door on purpose and any reasons she could imagine for this did not bode well for their future.

The cats sat in the doorway and discussed the meaning of all of this. They spoke in the way that pets and other animals do, with looks and body language, slight sounds and a sense that people just didn't grasp. Sasha

4

told Ava that maybe if she was a person she'd understand what had happened. She had never wanted to be a person before but, in their current situation, maybe it would help, to possibly understand, if only a little. Ava scoffed at this.

Soon Sasha dismissed these thoughts from her head. Being a person wouldn't help, how could it? One thing about people is they can't understand that for every situation there is something they can't understand. Sasha was fine with not understanding. They would just have to deal with whatever was happening the best they could.

Ava also realized that this was something they wouldn't be able to figure out. She'd quickly turned her attention to other matters. She seemed excited and wanted to go outside and explore. Sasha had a deep sense of foreboding and was much more cautious. She didn't know why she felt this way and questioned if it might be partly how she always felt when confronted with an open door.

In this way the cats were very different. When a door opened Ava would often make a run for it as if she were trying to make her escape, always eager to get outside and explore, always eager for adventure. As Ava would run for an open door, Sasha would slink away, her deep seated fear of being cold and hungry, huddling on the wrong side of a closed door, holding her back.

The cats' people often took them outside when the weather was nice. They had a long leash with a harness on each end. Ava loved these times and never wanted to go back inside. Sasha would soon be scratching at the door. Eventually one of her people would open the door for her. At this point she liked to sit down and look at them. Or, maybe, take one step inside then pause while looking around and sniffing the air. This was a good test for her people's fragile patience.

They eventually made their way outside, Sasha constantly lecturing Ava concerning the perils of the outside world and thoroughly not enjoying herself. Ava excitedly investigating every insect, twig, and leaf, watching as they tumbled in the crisp fall breeze, unconcerned with any perils of the outside world.

For a time they investigated around the house, never straying far from its base. There wasn't much to see, a few birds fluttered by, the cool breeze rustled the leaves that were just beginning to change color. But that was about it. No people, no animals, and very quiet. Not a single car came rumbling down the normally busy road in front of the house. Very odd, very strange. After a time they went back inside. Time being relative, it was much too short a time outside for Ava and much, much too long a time outside for Sasha.

Once inside they had a long cat talk. They discussed the missing people, the open door, the quiet, the fun and perils of exploring outside, and other cat interests. Kitties get very tired after long discussions, so after coming to no conclusions at all, they found comfortable spots and settled down for a bit of a cat nap, as cats often do.

In this way the next few days uneventfully passed with only a few things of note happening. The water bowl dried up and they began to drink unashamedly from the toilets. Their food bowl emptied but they were able to get at the large, nearly full cat food bag left in an open closet.

The cats were spending more time exploring the neighborhood. A storm had rolled through and today it was cool and rainy. They continued their explorations, lapping the clear clean water from puddles as they went.

Sasha commented on how much better this was than toilet water. Ava chuckled.

Besides the rain the storm had brought strong winds. This had caused a branch to crash through a window of a nearby home and the cats went over to explore. Sasha saw that they could easily gain access to the house, the branch had formed a natural bridge over the windowsill.

Sasha went first as Ava had been momentarily distracted by a leaf tumbling across the lawn. She slowly crept up the branch, poked her cute little head inside, looked and listened intently, thoroughly investigating her surroundings before she would commit to entering the house. As she surveyed the inside of the home she felt the branch tremble and was nearly knocked off the limb as Ava came pounding up the little bridge. Ava pushed past Sasha and lept, with nary a glance, deep into the darkened room. Sasha didn't like this, not at all. Ava had, so far, disregarded everything Sasha had said about being cautious.

They discovered maybe one thing of interest while exploring their previous neighbors home. A mouse scurried across the kitchen counter and disappeared behind a wall. Ava tried valiantly to catch the little critter. Sasha sat still on the floor and watched her sisters efforts.

This random encounter with the mouse got her thinking, the large bag of food back home would keep them fed for a while but it would eventually empty. Then, if the people hadn't returned, they would have to start hunting. Empty tummies would have to be filled.

Sasha knew her people would have never believed that she, being only a cat, was already thinking that far ahead. Cats weren't thinkers, she could almost hear them saying. At times it irked her to be treated like she was beneath the humans but they loved her and treated her well, so she forgave them.

What amazed her was that, from her point of view, it was the humans that were the limited thinkers. From her observations she doubted that they ever had anything that could be considered an intelligent thought. For instance, she knew deep down inside that she had all the intelligence she needed to survive indefinitely in the wild. She'd like to see one of her humans make it through a day without some hand held electronic device, a TV, and a vast array of kitchen appliances, at their immediate disposal. Survival, that was the lesson that living outside and sometimes being hungry, cold, and wet, had taught her.

Putting these thoughts aside Sasha focused her attention on Ava's clumsy efforts to catch the mouse. All cats were natural hunters but, like any God given skill, it could be honed, refined. And, if not used, maybe not totally lost, but a little too rusty to be counted on when your survival was at stake.

From all the noise and clatter that came from Ava's attempt to catch one little mouse Sasha knew there would be some needed training in Ava's future. She doubted Ava would be of a mood to listen to her lectures as she was so very excited to be out exploring and having adventures. That would change once her belly was empty, or so Sasha hoped.

The mouse disappeared in a small hole in the wall. Ava stuck a paw deep in the crevice to no avail. Sasha called for her sister, it was time to explore further. As they turned to leave Sasha thought she heard a raspberry type sound emanating from the mouse hole. This she chose to ignore.

The cats left the house and walked through the yards of a few more houses, looking for more broken windows or maybe an open door. As they explored they came across other strays. Many were not adjusting well. A couple dogs they met at first scared them. But Sasha saw the lost, sad look in their eyes and knew they were no threat. And when they spoke she understood.

The lost cats, the sad dogs, they all said the same things. Have you seen our people? They would describe them and talk as if they were the only people missing. Sasha would say that all of the people were gone but the response would always be the same. Yes, they would say in their animal ways, but have you seen our people and, once again, they would describe them.

They would describe tall ones and short ones, little girls and boys, men and women, moms' and dads'. Families, Sasha understood, that was what they described and all they cared about. They weren't worried about hunger or a dry bed, only their families. They were only lost and sad because they couldn't find their families. It was all rather heartbreaking.

One dog they met, an older Lab mix with a little gray peppering his muzzle, was kind to them and seemed to be aware of the situation, accepting that the people had gone and worried about this new life. They exchanged pleasantries with the old dog and soon parted. As the dog lumbered away he turned to them and told them to be safe, he didn't know if the people were coming back but, if they didn't, life for all of them, all of the former pets, could get a lot harder.

As they continued to explore, Sasha thought about the sad dogs and cats they'd met. The sadness was really a fear, if you thought about it. They were all so afraid and didn't understand why their families were gone. For now, sadness had sprung from their fear, when they started to become hungry that fear would produce something totally different, and this Sasha feared.

Sasha knew the humans thought of the cats as lesser creatures, not capable of the same range of emotions, or, for that matter, emotions at all. But to Sasha there were really only two emotions, fear and love. The humans seemed to think things were more complex than they really were. Did people actually have more than these emotions, fear and love? Wasn't their joy an expression of love, and their anger an expression of fear?

The humans, such strange creatures, angry, frustrated, tense, full of anxiety, mostly because they couldn't get what, or as much of, something they wanted. Which, in reality, is fear. But they didn't really think that way. From her experience they weren't actually deep thinkers, (when things got tough one of her humans always used to say 'drink on through it', no deep thinking there), so it was doubtful they'd make that connection. It was all pretty obvious to Sasha.

Sasha had watched people closely all her life. She noticed they did what they had to do to overcome their fear. They worked hard, lived life at a frantic pace, got the things or situations that they thought would overcome their fear of not having what they wanted only to find that there was something else just out of reach that they needed. By trying to overcome their fears of not having what they wanted they only compounded the problem by striving to get what they thought they needed. Sadly they were only feeding their fears, making them worse, and they didn't even realize it.

She once met one that understood. He worked at No Hope Shop on End of the Line Lane, making My Life is a Dead End signs for Mr Kiss My Ring And I'll Let You Live. But he was only doing that to survive and maybe eventually be able to buy his freedom. His only goal was to sit by a river and watch the water flow by, metaphorically speaking. From all of this Sasha concluded that hope is lost when wants matter. She was only concerned with needs.

Regardless of their many, many faults, she missed her people. Their strange bodies with so much ugly exposed skin. The way they awkwardly walked about on only two legs. So slow and clumsy. How they seemed to never stop wanting, more and more. Yes, these creatures really took some getting used to. With such glaring handicaps she was amazing they existed at all. Sasha thought that maybe some of these handicaps had helped them to survive but could not imagine how. She tried not to think too much about all of this, it was making her head spin, she just knew that she loved and missed them.

Ava called to her sister, Sasha had lagged behind as her little brain whirled with many thoughts. She sat on the cold ground and scratched at her ear, giving her head a nice good shake to clear it. Then got up and joined her sister, determined to not let her mind wander further. It wasn't safe to let one's mind wander at times like these. Survival, that had to be front and center in her brain from now on.

As they explored further from home they met more pets. After a time the cats began to notice changes in those they met. They stopped asking about their people. Other cats, for the most part, were avoiding them entirely, preferring to go off hunting on their own. The dogs were beginning to group up. At first this was fun to watch. They would run and play like there was no tomorrow. Dogs that had never been off of leashes, had never really had the chance to just run with others of their kind, were really enjoying their new found freedoms. But now they were becoming more aggressive, more dangerous.

The dogs were forming packs, some of which had already started to threaten and even fight with other packs. Ava and Sasha were just discussing the dangers of dog packs, as they walked along a damp sidewalk, when three dogs came trotting down the middle of the road towards them. The dogs, all much bigger than the cats, stopped suddenly when they noticed Sasha and Ava.

With a couple of loud barks and a flurry of paws digging at the pavement the dogs gave chase. The cats turned and ran. Instinctively they knew there was no way to out run the bigger animals so, before the dogs got too close, they shot up a nearby small tree. The dogs ran around the base of the tree barking at the cats and jumping, claws scraping at the bark of the trunk. The cats crouched low, well out of the dogs reach, and hissed threateningly at their tormentors.

It wasn't very long and the dogs tired of the game. Soon they trotted off, tails held high, evidently quite happy with themselves. From what Sasha had heard, the tones of the barks, the body language of the dogs, and other animal speak signs, it had been mostly play for the dogs, but it had been quite scary for the cats. It was a good lesson, especially for Ava, who was beginning to grasp that the outside world held some dangers. Sasha lectured her a little about what had happened and was encouraged that, for what was probably the first time, Ava seemed to actually listen.

Sasha told her that, when it came to dogs, they'd have to be much more careful. The small pack that had chased them up the tree seemed to be having fun but that could change once they got hungry. Ava had wondered why they would be hungry, they could just go home and eat out of their food bags. Sasha explained that they were lucky to have a food bag at home, not all pets would have that. They had seen cats hunting and dogs foraging out in the farmers fields nearby, maybe these former pets had nothing back at home to eat.

This was a perfect lead in to something Sasha had been wanting to make Ava aware of, since Ava was finally paying attention. So, as they made their way out of the tree and started for home, she continued the conversation. She asked Ava if she'd noticed that their food bag wasn't as full as it had been when their great adventure had started. Ava had not.

Sasha, with a furrowed brow, looked quizzically at her friend. How unaware, how naive, she thought. Sasha patiently explained that their food bag would not last forever, a concept that Ava, judging by her reaction, had never considered. When Sasha noticed the concern in Ava's eyes she comforted her somewhat by downplaying the seriousness of the situation, saying that they'd just have to start hunting more, and hunting was fun.

This excited Ava. They'd tried hunting, more for fun than anything, but Ava had been too noisy, and not patient enough, scaring the creatures they hunted away before they could get close. Sasha used this moment to convey to Ava that they needed to get more serious about hunting and pleaded with her to follow her example. Sasha was an excellent hunter and she hoped that she could quickly teach Ava some of the finer points of hunting. Ava was open to this idea. They would plan a hunting trip soon.

As they were speaking they came across the older black lab mix with the gray around his muzzle. He seemed cheerful enough and was glad to see them again. He had a companion, a small white fluffy girl dog that growled fiercely at the cats. The bigger dog nudged her and told her they were his friends. The smaller dog soon quit growling but told the lab mix that dogs didn't have cats for friends. She went rambling on, something about there not being friends anymore, there were only packs and she wouldn't be part of a pack that ran with cats. They needed more in their pack, she wanted more, but not cats.

So the bigger dog and the cats stood and chatted for a few minutes while the fluffy little girl slunk over to the base of a big maple tree, sat down, and commenced to pout.

The lab had seen them having trouble with the dogs and agreed they looked like they were just having fun, but he worried that the packs were getting more aggressive and again warned the cats to be careful. He looked over his shoulder at his companion then back at the cats. He told the cats that he figured the two of them would probably soon be part of a larger pack. The little dog was going to join one, there was nothing he could do about that, and he didn't want to be alone. He said he'd do what he could to help the cats but told them not to approach if he was part of a larger pack. He was getting older and wasn't in good enough shape to be a leader. Young, tough dogs led packs, and that kind of dog didn't listen to old dogs like him.

Soon they parted ways, the fluffy white dog giving them a sour look, and, with nose and tail both high in the air, she pranced away. The big dog smiled at them, in that way that animals smile at each other, and went with her.

Another day was drawing to a close as the cats entered their home. They'd exercised more caution than usual so the trip took longer. Even though there seemed to be no more threats Sasha had wanted to show Ava how to secretly move about. So they kept close to cover as best they could, walking low, hiding in bushes, trying not to be seen. No matter that there wasn't anyone around to see them, Sasha just figured they needed the practice. To Ava it was all a great game and she enjoyed herself thoroughly.

They ate dinner from the food bag and went to the living room to groom and talk. They had a very good conversation and Sasha was encouraged that Ava seemed to be taking the talk about hunting and hiding much more seriously. It apparently took only one bad encounter with the dogs to give her a much needed attitude adjustment, one that could save her life, thought Sasha.

Chapter 2

One morning, as the cats left the house to sit on the front porch, a familiar Robin lit in the big maple tree in their front yard. His name was Clarence and he seemed to enjoy chatting with the cats from time to time. It seemed odd as cats and birds are often considered mortal enemies. This relationship seemed to do away with the old stereotypes.

It was a cool morning but it looked like it was going to be a sunny day. A storm had blown past and a couple sunny days had dried the ground and made outside adventuring much more comfortable. Although the sun wouldn't completely lift the chill from the autumn day it still felt good on their backs.

Clarence greeted them and inquired as to their general well being. They exchanged pleasantries and talked about the weather. Clarence mentioned that he and his family would be heading south in a few more weeks and hoped to see the cats next spring. Secretly he had his doubts. How could pets survive the harsh realities of a Michigan winter without the helping hand of their people? He didn't talk about any of this of course, he liked the cats and there was nothing he could do to help them, probing the issue would only create unrest.

This morning the robin had decided to tell the cats the reason he had sought them out after the people left. The story began on a early summer evening a couple years ago. It was warm with a slight breeze and Clarence was a young robin still in the nest. The cats were amazed to hear that the nest Clarence spoke of was here in this maple tree. They were even more amazed when Clarence pointed out the very nest where he had entered this world. It was tattered and old looking, weathered and unattended as it was. And only visible now that many of the yellowing and reddish leaves had fallen from the tree.

Clarence explained that he had been anxious to leave the nest. He seemed more eager than any of his siblings and was constantly climbing onto the edge of the nest and flapping his wings. His mother would often shoo him back down and try and explain that he needed to be a little stronger before he left the nest. There were many dangers on the ground and little robins that couldn't fly would be in serious trouble.

Clarence was young and did not heed his mother's words. He felt no fear as he clung to the edge of the nest that fateful evening. His mother and father were off frantically hunting insects and worms for their ever hungry brood.

The breeze had picked up as the sun went down, which was odd in of itself. Clarence stretched out his wings and gave a hearty flap just as a gust of wind rustled the leaves. The breeze caught his wings and he lost his grip on the edge of the nest. And away went Clarence, the first of his clan to leave the nest, never to return.

He fluttered and flapped and confidently proclaimed himself to be flying. When, in truth, all he was doing was prolonging his fall. His siblings, none the wiser, peered out of the nest and cheered him on, until he thudded to the ground, knocking the breath out of him. Then there was silence.

After a few moments he called up to his brothers and sisters and let them know he was okay. One of them called back down and told him to hurry and get back in the nest, mom and dad would be home soon and he'd be in big trouble. Clarence fluttered his wings and hopped about, gaining but a few inches of altitude before stumbling back down to the ground.

It was silent again, Clarence wouldn't be coming back to the nest tonight, or ever again. Instinctively they all knew, even the confident Clarence, that their mother had been right. He was too young to leave the nest. Birds that left the nest too early don't survive. This thought was beginning to creep into their little minds when the mother returned.

She noticed Clarence right away and dropped the worm she'd been carrying, much to the delight of the worm. Broken hearted the mother swooped down to comfort him. She quickly put her feelings aside and guided Clarence over to some nearby bushes. He was able to hop/fly into the low hanging branches and take cover.

His mom spoke to him, encouraging him to be brave. He would need to stay put, make the bush his home, try not to draw attention to himself. She and dad would bring him food and he would grow strong and soon be able to fly away. The doubt was evident to all that heard.

With the mention of food she flew off and grabbed the very worm she'd earlier dropped, much to the chagrin of the worm. Clarence ate and stepped deeper into the bush as mom flew off. She would stay with Clarence as much as she could but the rest of her young needed tending too.

As night wore on a nearby door opened and out stepped a person. Clarence cowered in fear. His parents were sleeping in the tree with his family, only he noticed. The person sat in a chair only a few feet from Clarence, he had no idea what they were doing. Maybe they couldn't sleep and it was a nice, warm night. Hopefully they would sit for a while, enjoying the evening, then just go away.

After what seemed like a very long time, but in reality was only a few minutes, Clarence watched the person get up and open the door to go inside. To his horror, as the door opened, a terrifying looking cat slipped outside and went under the chair. The person didn't seem to notice, went inside, and closed the door. The cat went up to the door and stared at it, perplexed, for the longest time.

Clarence heard the cat meow that she'd just wanted to come out and cuddle with her person and to please please please let her back in, she was very afraid.

Clarence stopped telling the story and told his audience that the cat at the door was Sasha. Sasha knew this but for whatever reason had not brought it up. The audience had grown as a few of Clarence's bird friends had perched in the tree. There was a cardinal, a sparrow, and a loud blue jay which laughed when he heard of Sasha's fear. She was embarrassed but fought not to show it.

Back to the story, Clarence admitted to being greatly afraid. He wanted to call out to mom and dad but remembered he wasn't supposed to draw attention to himself. He sat on his branch, as very still as a very little bird could be.

Soon he noticed the scary cat sniffing the air and looking his way. He knows the next part of the story took several minutes but at the time it seemed that in only an instant the cat had come his way and discovered him in the bush, their faces only inches apart. Clarence wanted to scream out to his mom and dad but he couldn't make a sound. He soiled the ground beneath him.

The cat just looked at him, no expression whatsoever. Clarence was sure this was the end, he closed his eyes. Then Sasha spoke to him, telling him not to be afraid and that she wouldn't hurt him. Clarence opened his eyes, surprised to hear the cat speaking to him, shocked to hear the words that were spoken.

Clarence admitted that he broke down and cried at that time, overcome with sadness, fear, and finally relief. No one laughed.

As he sat in the bush he told Sasha his story, highlighting his foolishness at not listening to his mother. He was afraid for himself but also very sad because he had upset his little family so very much. Sasha, in an attempt to comfort the little bird, told him it was okay to be afraid and sometimes fear could help us. She told of her fears stemming from her youth and being left outside and how those experiences were helping her now. They chatted for a long time and they comforted each other.

Early in the morning, so very early it might not even be considered morning as the sun had not yet broken over the eastern horizon, the door opened again. A different person stepped out and whispered the name Sasha. She quickly wished Clarence all the luck in the world, said her goodbyes, and ran to her person, expressing her happiness with many mew's and purrs.

And that, concluded Clarence, was how a cat and a bird became friends. There were many cheers from the crowd that now included several birds, a squirrel and a rabbit. All were appreciative of a good story with a happy ending. Life was hard enough and full of sad stories, the little creatures of the world had no interest in stories that weren't happy.

After a time the crowd dispersed, Clarence wished the cats a good day and swooshed away. The cats, after enjoying such a good story and even better company, felt very peaceful and serene. Ava yawned, Sasha copied. The story time had tired them out and they both decided, as cats often do, that it was time for a nap.

Over the next few weeks Sasha helped her willing student, Ava, to become a much better hunter. They had started going out mostly at night, this suited them both as cats are naturally nocturnal and at their best when it's dark out. Excellent night vision and natural stealth gave them a big advantage over their prey. Just as importantly, night hunting kept them safe from dogs, who only seemed to be out during the day.

At first the cats hunted bushes and overgrowths at the edge of yards, then the nearby farmers fields. The little neighborhood they lived in was surrounded by farmers fields. Fields that hadn't been harvested as all the people were gone. The food left behind drew in the rodent population.

They were having pretty decent luck hunting rodents in these areas and Ava was progressing nicely. She had watched Sasha closely and had improved her patients and dramatically improved her stealth. Although not yet as adept as Sasha she'd caught her fair share of mice. The food bag would last a lot longer if they continued to have more success hunting, thought Sasha.

As it got colder they found that houses were becoming a better place to hunt. There were only a few nearby that they could get into, through a door or window that had been left open or somehow been opened, but these were teeming with mice. The colder weather motivated the rodents to look for warmer places and, with lots of people food left behind, there was no shortage of sustenance. Thus the houses were becoming rodent breeding grounds.

This night they were walking around one such house. Even outside they could hear the faint rustling of rodents inside the house. They found places where mouse smell was strong, and saw their little tracks in the mud. There were small openings the rodents used to enter the house, but none were near big enough for cats.

At the back of the house they got a bit of luck. A screen door at ground level appeared to not be fully shut. Sasha, being the master of doors, got to work.

She had always been good with doors. She'd learned that she could stand against some doors, and if they weren't latched, her weight would push them open. Others she'd figured out that by reaching under them and hooking her paw around against the backside, she'd often been able to pull doors open.

With this door she tried the latter. At first she had no success. She enlisted Ava's help and they dug at the ground in front of the door. Leaves and other debris had piled up here, maybe clearing some of that out would help. It did. A few more minutes of digging and grasping at the door and she was able to pry it open, only to find a second door, much more solid then the first, in the way.

She tried pulling, she tried pushing, the door did not budge. She looked up at the door knob, well, maybe not a knob, this one was different, one she hadn't seen before, it was more like a lever that stuck out to the side, parallel to the ground.

Sasha had often observed her people using door knobs and had reasoned that they had something to do with opening doors, but she was never able to figure them out. On occasion she would jump and slap at the knobs, but nothing would happen. If her people saw her they would laugh and holler for anyone else in the house to come see the funny cat antics. This pissed her off and she'd try even harder. Of course, this would frustrate her even more. Eventually one of the people would open the door for her, not what she'd wanted, and she would slink off in the opposite direction. To top it all off the people would call after her, telling her the door was open, why are you going the other way, and commenting about how silly cats were.

She remembered being angry about this as she sat there staring at this door knob, no, door lever. She sure wished she could go back to those days when all she had to be upset about were things like not being able to open a door or her people laughing at her.

Ava gave her a nudge and asked what they would do now. Snapping back to the moment Sasha decided she'd give her old door knob strategy a try. Maybe it would work, this thing looked really different. She had no idea how it happened but, on her very first try, she jumped up and grabbed at the handle and heard a very satisfying click. The door opened ever so slightly. She stood up on her hind legs, put her front paws on the door, and it swung easily inward.

This house hunt was particularly successful, Sasha thought that it wouldn't be long and they would no longer need the food bag at all. After the hunt they left the house and headed home.

Once home they revelled in the hunting success they were now having. They'd come a long way and felt much more independent. They spoke about their people and what they might think about this turn of events. Ava wanted to tell them that the cats no longer needed them, they were fine on their own.

They were silent for a few minutes. Soon Sasha began to tell Ava about a memory she had. It was when the man and little girl would play the board game Sorry and set a place for each cat. She remembered how the little girl would hold a disgruntled Sasha in her lap and show her those meaningless cards and move a piece on the board for her. She'd squirm and try to get away but secretly loving the attention and being included in her family's fun time. They both laughed when Sasha recalled how Ava's main participation would be to jump up on the table to steal one of the pawns and scamper away with her loot.

Even when their people were just sitting watching the idiot box the cats would be with them, they'd all spend their time together. Relaxing, lounging, playing games, eating, they were together. Yes, she told her sister, we don't need them, we can get by on our own, but I miss them. Ava did too. The cats went to bed with wonderful memories swirling around in their little heads.

The next morning dawned bright and cold, the sunshine glistening off the frosted grass. This morning Clarence came to see the cats. He chattered in the front tree until the cats awoke and came out to greet him.

He had come to bid them farewell, today was the day he was heading south. He'd previously told them all about this coming day and explained that this was something his kind did every year. Not all birds were like him and some birds that Clarence had introduced to the cats would be staying behind. They would check in with the cats from time to time.

The cats knew this day was coming but that didn't soften the blow, they'd both come to enjoy their chats with Clarence. Clarence was looking forward to the warmer climate that he was heading to, the cats laughed and said they were jealous. They all chuckled but each of them, even Ava, knew that soon the cold would be no laughing matter.

Clarence told the cats they were looking well and the cats talked a little about their successful hunts, being sure to mention it was only rodents they were after. This gave Clarence hope that maybe they would be okay, maybe they would make it through the winter.

They spoke for a few more minutes then wished each other the best of luck and off Clarence flew. Clarence, as he flew away, was glad that, as the cats had talked about hunting, they'd only talked about mice!

Chapter 3

The cats had become mostly nocturnal, sleeping the days away, venturing out to hunt and explore at night. This day Ava woke to a bright, late afternoon sun shining in her eyes. Anxious for adventure she woke her sister and soon convinced Sasha to follow her outside. Sasha was a reluctant companion, not liking the idea of being outside, exposed, while the sun was still up. It was a cold day, but the sun felt warm on their backs, perfect weather for two cats to go exploring. To Ava the only weather she didn't care for was rain, she could suffer cold.

Ava wanted to explore a little further from home today. Sasha expressed her concern and requested they proceed with caution. Caution wasn't something Ava was very familiar with, nor cared much about, but she had been learning so she respected Sasha's wishes and they slinked off, slow and low. Ava didn't mind slinking off, slinking was something that came natural to cats, and she enjoyed the intensity of the moment.

They worked their way around the neighbors' house and across the yard, which was now more of a field as they were completely concealed within the tall grass. They came to a wooden fence, the kind with horizontal planks with gaps between, plenty of space for a cat to crawl through.

The fence was a faded white and in a state of disrepair. Some planks had fallen out of the posts at one end or the other, making odd angles to the other planks. Others had fallen out completely. The cats had noticed a few broken people things. Without people to repair them, they would stay that way. But this fence was obviously already in a state of disrepair, neglected by the previous owner long before the people had left.

This worked out to the cats advantage as they prowled along. Stepping on one of the planks Ava scared out a small pack of rodents that had been hiding underneath. The cats gave chase, and with their much improved and refined hunting skills, were soon able to catch a late afternoon meal. They dined on the banks of a small pond that had been hidden from view by overgrowth.

After they ate the cats made their way down a slight bank to the water's edge, where they drank their fill. The water had a lot of thin ice cover but was open for a couple of feet from shore. They walked along the water's edge and came to a small wooden walkway that had been built part way along one side of the pond. They hopped up on the deck boards and strolled along.

Near the end of the little wooden path they noticed that, where the wood slightly overhung the pond, the ice cover had come nearly to shore. It would be a simple matter to leap out on the ice and explore.

Sasha, watching Ava closely, asked her if she was seriously considering going out there. Ava chuckled and responded that there wasn't a chance of that happening. She was curious, as cats often are, but she wasn't about to risk getting wet when there wasn't anything out there but ice and water, although, for some reason she couldn't explain, she did find the little pond fascinating.

They had stopped at the end of the little walkway and, as they gazed down at the water, they saw something large move slowly under the thin ice. Ava quickly jumped off the platform and scooted down the to the waters edge, Sasha right behind her, calling out to be careful.

At the water's edge Ava sat still, gazing out into its depths. Soon, whatever it was, had circled around and was heading right towards her. Although her cat senses weren't sounding any alarms she instinctively crouched lower as she watched the creature slowly approach. Sasha backed a few steps away but did not scold her sister.

As it got closer Ava saw it was a large fish, much too large for the cats to consider as prey. It had a big body that tapered down to a small head. The snout had several whiskers around a small, down turned mouth.

The fish swam up to Ava, so close now they were nearly touching noses, and asked the cat, in that same animal language that all the creatures used, if she had seen its person.

Ava smiled but took a moment to answer, having been surprised at the abruptness of the question and that the fish had spoken at all. After regaining her composure she explained to the fish that all of the people were missing. Sasha, overcome by her own curiosity, approached the fish and told it they had no idea where all the people had gone and if they were ever coming back.

The fish just stared at the cats, its large eyes slowly moving back and forth between them. It was silent for so long that Sasha began to think it wasn't smart enough to understand what the cats had said. Just as she was about to begin trying to further explain the fish spoke. There's more?

The cats looked at the fish with puzzled expressions on their fuzzy little faces. Questioningly they looked at each other then back at the fish. In animal speak they simultaneously asked the fish what it meant by 'there's more'. The fish replied that he only knew of his person, an odd looking creature with a tuft of gray hair on its head. It was the only creature that came to the pond that had but two legs. It was so odd to see, all the other creatures were long like the fish, but the person, it reached straight up like the reeds that grew along the pond's edge. Such an odd looking creature.

Sometimes the fishes would see the person walking slowly around the pond carrying a small bag. They knew what this meant and would swim over to greet the person. The person would make comforting sounds and toss out handfuls of the most yummy food. The fish would happily gobble it all up.

They didn't need the food, they found plenty to eat on the bottom of the pond, but the food was really good, much better than their normal diet. And it was a special time, when the person came. It talked to the fishes as it fed them, and, although they didn't understand what the person was saying, as it apparently didn't know animal speak, it made them feel special. It was hard to feel special when all you did was swim around a small pond and eat whatever fell to the bottom.

The other creatures that came to the pond all had four legs and they never stopped to talk, with the two cats being the only exception. So the fish enjoyed the person and had come to miss it. Again the fish asked the cats if they'd seen its person.

By this time several more of the big fish had swam over and were staring up forlornly at the cats. Sasha again explained, slowly, that the people were all missing and they hadn't seen them. Seeing the blank looks she changed tact and simply said that no, they hadn't see the fishes person. This was met with sad fish groans, a couple turned and slowly swam away. Sasha thought that lumbered away would be a more accurate description of their movements but didn't think the word fit for the swimming of a fish.

Ava continued to stare at the fishes that remained, incredulous at their inability to understand what Sasha had said. She asked them if they understood that there were many many people, too many to even count, and that they were all missing. The fishes blankly returned her gaze, plainly they thought the cat mad. Many many people, what kind of foolishness was this, everyone knew there was only the one person, they hadn't even thought there was a plural to the word.

The cats glanced knowingly at each other. It was the kind of look they shared when their person, the man, would tell one of his silly stories, one of which popped in Ava's head. She'd heard him many times describe a man with two beer cans in the front pockets of his flannel shirt then saying 'look at the cans on that dude', and laugh laugh laugh. She'd never understood the humor, but this was how both cats felt about the fish, they looked at each other then back to the blank stare of the fish. Plainly this discussion had ended.

They told the fish they'd come let it know if they saw its person. The fish thanked them and, surprisingly, asked them to stop by and visit again someday. It got lonely swimming around this same old pond everyday with no one to talk to except the other fishes. Swimming a little closer he told the cats, in a low voice so as not to be overheard, that the other fish were kind of stupid and weren't capable of a decent conversation. The cats chuckled then bade the fish good day and he swam away.

Turning from the pond Sasha and Ava made their way up the gentle slope of the bank to the yard/field above. Unsure of exactly where they were Ava sat up on her haunches and poked her head above the tall grass. A short distance to their left was the familiar fence, they headed that way.

Walking towards the fence they talked about their new fish friend and laughed a little. It was actually kind of interesting, meeting a fish. They'd met some before, the little girl person had a fish tank in her room, but those fish never spoke to them, they just hid. The cats continued to chat as they walked. Ava told Sasha the story she'd just recalled about the man that lived with them that had popped in her head. Sasha smiled, remembering his laughter, and thought to herself that Ava must miss her people more then she lets on, having memories like that.

Hearing Ava's nostalgic story made Sasha want to tell one. She relayed a memory that Ava had already heard many times, but the mood was light and she smiled as Sasha spoke. Another story about the man, how when something bad would happen he'd grab a beer and sit on the sofa and, as the cats sat and quizzically looked at him, he'd impart what he thought was great wisdom on them. His favorite saying for such a time was 'isn't it funny how one day you can shit three times, the next day you don't shit at all, and the 3rd day your life turns to shit!'. And then laugh laugh laugh. The cats thought this total nonsense, they both knew that sometimes your bowel movements weren't regular but how did that turn your life to poopy? They had both attempted to get him to explain further but he didn't understand animal speak and he'd just pat them on their heads, a little too firmly, and go on about his business.

Both cats were quite cheerful as they walked, thinking about their new friend and remembering old people stories. It was good to make new friends, and even better to remember old ones. On they went, smiling as they walked.

Once they reached the fence Sasha went to the right, Ava left. They turned and looked at each other. Sasha had turned towards home, it was late and getting colder. She wanted to go home, maybe nap a little, then find a house to hunt that night.

Ava protested, it wasn't dark yet, the sun still warmed them, albeit slightly, and the fence ended just up ahead, she could see it. She finally talked Sasha into exploring till they reached the end of the fence, then they could go home.

Unfortunately for Sasha the fence ended at the bank of a creek, something Ava had never seen before. The cats paused at the top of the bank, curiously looking about. Sasha was nervous, the creek, lots of trees, anything could be hiding here.

The ground sloped away to the slowly moving water below. Before Sasha could voice her concerns Ava had already began moving down the bank thinking of a cool drink and what she might see in the water. Sasha, ever the cautious kitty, kept to her perch at the top of the bank. There were a lot of tall trees lining the back, and, combined with all the thick scrub brush, gave the place an eerie feel. Something was triggering Sasha's internal warning bells.

As Ava lapped at the water on the edge of the creek and Sasha sniffed at the brisk autumn air there was a disturbing rustling in the nearby scrub brush. This attracted Sasha's attention but Ava was oblivious. Then there was a low rumbling growl which instantly drew the attention of both cats. They both looked in the general direction of the noises and each saw the head of a tan and white dog as it poked out of the bushes.

He was a large dog with a thick jaw. His gaze locked in on Ava, who's hackles immediately rose, at the creeks bank. Sasha sank lower to the earth, apparently unnoticed.

The dog took a couple of brisk steps forward, emerging from his hiding place and zeroing in on Ava. The dog did not look friendly at all, it took another couple of threatening steps towards Ava, the situation looked dire.

Sasha loved her little sister and tried to care for her. Even though Ava was a little older and somewhat bigger Sasha realized, even if Ava did not, that she depended on her. Sasha felt responsible for her sister and took great pains to help and guide her through this troubling new world. Now she was nearly panicked at the prospect of losing her dear friend. When the dog had moved forward it was clear he was preparing to make a charge at Ava.

The big dog crouched and tightened his haunches. Just as he was about to spring down the bank Sasha gave out a loud hiss causing him to stop and spin to face Sasha. Sasha inched backwards to the base of a tall tree, ready to turn and quickly climb to safety. The tan and white dog, sensing this, turned his attention back to Ava at the water's edge.

Sasha didn't know what else to do, she had tried to draw off the dogs attention but he was a savvy and savage animal, and he knew which cat was the easier prey. Sasha watched in horror as the dog tensed and sprung forward, bursting down the bank after Ava. Sasha took a couple of quick steps forward, everything happened so fast she hardly had time to react.

The dog, jaws opened wide, lunged at Ava who had turned sideways, fur puffed up, back arched. All appeared lost. Nowhere to run, nowhere to hide, a house cat with no experience dealing with dangerous situations, was lost.

Then the most amazing thing happened. At the very last moment Ava sprung straight up in the air, as only a cat, with its powerful hind quarters, could do. The dog attempted to brake, twisting and contorting, but it was no use. He shot under Ava and plunged into the cold water. He hit a deep pool and was, for an instant, totally submerged.

At that moment Sasha screamed "RUNNNNNNN" and Ava, as soon as her little paws hit the ground, ran up the bank as if she were shot out of a cannon, blowing by Sasha.

They raced through the tall grass, following the fence line, heading for home. They came up to the neighbors house before they heard a terrible howl well behind them. They didn't give any thought as to why the dog was so far behind them, they just ran.

The dog, in his haste to get turned around and give chase, had stumbled on slippery rocks while in the water, fell a couple times, made it to the bank, slipped and fell once more in the mud, blindly ran full tilt up the bank, crashed into, and became entangled in, bushes at the top, finally emerging into the yard beyond, at which point he'd given a great howl of frustration. By this time any rational dog would have realized the cats were long gone but the tan and white dog's anger got the best of him, he'd not let two house cats show him up. He bounded out into the yard, caught their scent at the fence and gave chase.

The cats soon reached home, but Sasha yelled at Ava to keep going. She had experienced being chased by predators before and didn't want to lead the big dog directly to their forever home. She led them up to one house then quickly backtracked. At another house they went in through a broken front window, ran through several rooms, up and down stairs then exited the house through a back door. They approached a couple more houses, went in and out of another through the same window, then climbed up onto the front porch of a house and jumped into the nearby branches of a large tree.

Out of breath, eyes wide with fear, they settled in the tree and waited.

The dog, while running along the fence row, had to pause a couple of times as the cat scent went in different directions. He followed it once and came to a pond, looking in the water he saw a large fish swimming his way. The fish started to say something about a person but the dog turned and spun out, sending clumps of dirt into the pond, scaring the fish away. How rude, thought the fish.

The tan and white dog ran up the bank, back to the fence, he followed it to a house, picked up the cat scent, crossed some more yard and emerged into a small neighborhood. He ran about, sniffing up to one house then another, getting more and more frustrated. Eventually he was in a pure rage, hurrying from house to house, barking and howling, slobber flying all about.

The cats saw the big dog running amok, he never came so close as to worry the cats. It was getting dark now and eventually the crazy creature ran out of steam. He stood in the middle of the road, five or six houses away from where the cats hid, and looked about, his head turning quickly from side to side.

Soon his head stopped moving and the cats thought they heard a sigh. He turned and, as darkness fell, slunk away into the night, away from the cats.

It was some time before the cats dared leave the tree and when they finally did it was only to leap down to the porch roof they'd entered the tree from. Here they hid in the darkness, looking far and wide, with their excellent night vision, for any signs of danger. They probably sat there for an hour, not speaking, only watching, listening, occasionally sniffing at the air. This had been the greatest scare they had experienced, what a great adventure thought Ava. Sasha was mortified.

Chapter 4

After their narrow escape from the tan and white dog the cats were much more cautious. They resolved to stay inside during daytime, only venturing out at night. They'd talked about this before but this time they really meant it.

The air was quite cool this time of year. This was causing a change in the cats, something Sasha recognized from her early days as and outdoor kitty. Their fur was beginning to thicken. This would be a big help for nighttime hunting as the nights got colder and colder.

This night they went out later than usual and they had a bit of a tough time hunting. They were trying a new house and, although there seemed to be plenty of rodents, they were very adept at avoiding the cats. It was like the mice had a signal and once one of them spotted the cats all the others were made aware and took refuge in small places. This was not the norm. Perhaps another hunter had been here and now these mice were more wary.

The cats resorted to using teamwork. Ava would slam into a hiding spot, scaring rodents out the other side where Sasha would be waiting. Eventually they had a decent, if not totally fulfilling, meal. Dawn was breaking before they left the house.

As the day began to lighten they headed back home, looking this way and that with every step they took. They'd taken too long to hunt that night. Having been so deeply involved with the hunt neither of them had noticed the coming of the dawn. They were compensating for being out during the day by being extra cautious as they headed back home. They were behaving more and more like wild animals, very aware of their surroundings and determined not to let any threats sneak up on them.

Ava especially was a changed animal, stealthily sneaking through the grass like a seasoned wild cat. It was a welcome sight for Sasha who had been having trouble convincing Ava to exercise caution. The big tan and white dog had taught Ava a valuable lesson, one that Sasha had failed to impart. Luckily without any serious consequence.

Sasha thought such is life, sometimes we are lucky to learn a valuable lesson without any great consequence. At these times we must be very thankful, remembering what happened and how lucky we were to avoid what could have happened. Thinking of her missing humans, again she speculated if thoughts like these ever occurred to them. She doubted it.

Concentrating mightily, reacting to every sight, sound, and smell, the cats slowly snuck back towards home. And that is why they both nearly jumped out of their skins when a smallish, light brown, creature sprung out from behind the maple tree in their front yard, only a couple feet in front of them.

The animal saw the cats and froze, as did the cats. The little creature timidly greeted them then bounced back behind the tree. The cats looked at each other, then back at the little guy who had scurried a few feet up the tree trunk and was looking at them while upside down, clinging to the tree, with his neck at an odd angle. The cats both recognized him, he was the little acrobat that was constantly entertaining the cats and their people as he attempted to raid the bird feeder.

The squirrel seemed to recognize them also and bid them a good morning and the cats replied in kind. Ava asked him how he was and mentioned that she enjoyed his company at the bird feeder.

The little squirrel fidgeted this way and that, rapidly chattering his reply, telling the cats how he missed the feeder and wondering why the people stopped filling it. He went on to say that he had enjoyed their company too and often questioned why they didn't come out to play. He mentioned that he sometimes felt like they would play too rough and that is why he sometimes resorted to teasing them. The cats remembered how he would scamper back and forth on the window ledge as they would paw at the glass.

The cats again exchanged glances and giggled a little at the squirrels' jittery behaviour. They apologized if they seemed a little too aggressive but it was their nature, and forgave him his teasing as they deserved to be treated in such a way if they weren't going to play nice. They told the squirrel the people had left and they didn't know when, or if, they'd be coming back. The squirrel gave pause to his jittery movements and told the cats that this wasn't good news, not good at all. After all, who would now fill the feeders?

The squirrel asked them what they were doing out and about during the day. He'd not seen them out in a long time. He slept at night and assumed that that was when the cats went prowling about. They told him a lie, that they had been out exploring a little longer than usual, they didn't want to use the word 'hunt'. They returned the inquiry, asking the squirrel what he was doing today.

The squirrel chattered on and on about nuts and just how many would be enough and would there be enough time and would there be enough places to hide the nuts. You can never have enough nuts you know. Ava mentioned that if you had more than you could possibly ever eat wouldn't that be enough?

But Mr Squirrel wasn't derailed a bit, he told Ava that maybe possibly, possibly maybe, but it might still not be enough, maybe. It was all in animal speak but very fast. Ava and Sasha got the gist of it, he was going to gather nuts all day, every day, no matter what.

For some reason this exchange made Sasha again think of the missing humans, they were kind of like their new friend Mr Squirrel. Always gathering, never having enough, even when they obviously had too much. Hurrying this way and that to gather something else, something bigger, something shinier. She just could never understand this frantic pace of life chosen by people and that she was witnessing in Mr Squirrel. It seemed that their entire lives were wrapped up in gathering and only a few differences could she see in Mr Squirrel's behavior and that of the people she'd witnessed. If Mr Squirrel started gathering shinny things to show to his friends and neighbors and then hired other squirrels to gather nuts and shiny things for him, well, then Sasha doubted she'd be able to tell the difference at all.

After a short time they said their goodbyes and turned to go home, it was definitely time for a cat nap. Mr Squirrel said he was going to gather nuts.

Just as they started to walk away from each other, he turned and, in an entirely different, completely serious manner, in animal speak he said to his new friends, watch out for the dogs. Watch closely, they have a leader now and they are gathering. Oh my but these are dangerous times. And with that he scampered off, returning to his previous manner of speech as he chattered about gathering nuts.

The cats wondered if the leader was the big tan and white dog they'd met at the creek, Sasha figured he was. He was the first former pet they'd met that had shaken off the sadness of losing his people and adapted to the new life. She could see him, in her mind's eye, bullying the other dogs to forget the old way and follow him on a new path. This wasn't good, not at all. One mean dog was trouble but a pack was, well, obviously much worse. She watched the squirrel rush this way and that, seeming to look in all directions at once, and, as he passed from her field of vision, thought what a dark omen you've brought, Mr Squirrel.

Chapter 5

The house is cold this day as the cats cuddle for warm in their favorite plush red chair. The only thing disturbing their peaceful slumber is Ava occasionally digging at her fur, she's getting a little bit of a flea problem. Sasha figures they picked up the fleas from all the rodent hunting they have been doing.

It's beginning to get a little dark outside and Sasha got up to peer out a window. Another storm went through today and the clouds are still dark and menacing.

They went outside and continued their explorations, lapping the clear, clean rain water from puddles as they went. It's been getting colder and there's been some snow but today it had warmed up some and rained instead. 'Warmed up some' was misleading, Sasha thought. The beginning of winter was maybe a week or two away, Sasha needed no calendar to tell her that. Rain on the verge of winter was cold, it chilled you to the bone. It made everything damp and wet, and the dampness hung in the air like a wet coat, chilling its wearer.

As the front had blown through it had been very windy. As they explored the cats noticed a couple more homes with doors ajar. A broken branch had crashed through a window at another home they previously had no access to. Sasha made mental notes of these homes, more hunting grounds. Once open the doors weren't being closed, once broken the windows weren't being fixed, there were no people. None, after all this time, not a single person had they found.

They went inside the first home that they had gained access to after the people had left. They hadn't hunted this place in a while as there were so many other places to explore. The house was teeming with rodents. Cabinet doors were ajar, boxes of crackers and pasta and other assorted dry goods were scattered, it was quite a mess. They took the rodents by surprise. It was a good day to be a cat, but not so good if you were a mouse.

All of these empty homes with plenty of food left inside, they were quickly becoming rodent infested. Many houses the cats still could not get in to, but, as they poked around outside they could hear the rodents scurrying about inside. They could smell the mouse entrances but found them way too small for a cat.

As the weather turned colder the mice had begun to stream out of the fields to take advantage of the abandoned homes with ample supplies of food, it was mouse heaven. It only takes about three weeks for mice to have babies, and they were breeding like crazy. With people gone, and all that people food left behind, a couple months and their population was getting out of control. This was working out to the great advantage of the cats. In fact, unknown to the cats, the first litters that had come along after the people had left were nearly ready to start having babies of their own. The mice grew fast and strong, an unhindered food supply and plenty of safe shelter helping them along. The cats had been able to fill their bellies with hunting alone. This enabled them to leave an emergency supply of food in the large bag at home.

As they explored the rain turned to a mixture of rain and snow. As it fell to the ground the snow mostly melted, leaving slight traces of white here and there on blades of grass. Ava had never been outside in the snow and Sasha told her that there would be times this winter that they found it very difficult, if not impossible, to get through the snow and make it to one of their hunting grounds. Ava, having spent many a winter comfortably lounging in her favorite chair, remembered watching the snow pile up. She believed Sasha.

For this reason Sasha had discouraged any eating at the food bag. Sasha had thought it would be a problem, convincing Ava to keep an emergency supply of food, but it wasn't. Ava's first thought nearly every evening was to go outside and hunt. She was having the time of her life. But she also saw the specter of the coming snows and imagined there would be several days to come that she and her sister would prefer to stay inside, snacking lightly from the bag.

On their nightly hunts the cats took to extending their range, but always, when the hunt was over, they returned home. Their forever home was still home to the cats, they felt comfortable and safe, even with the front door slightly propped open. Their house, although cold, was still clean and dry. A few rodents had snuck in but they were quickly dispatched. The flea problem had worsened and that was a concern, but other then that they felt fairly comfortable with their situation.

As they hunted further and further from home they, of course, found more homes to hunt. The plan, per Sasha, who was thinking of the cold and deep snows of winter, was to let the rodent populations build up in the houses closer to home. She'd learned to look ahead when she'd been an outdoor kitty, but a cat being a cat, she couldn't see all the possibilities. One problem she didn't foresee was that the exploding rodent population would literally eat themselves out of house and home, forcing them to abandon houses and brave the cold of winter in search of new food sources.

This was a problem for another time. This night they explored far and came across a likely house. The front entrance had two doors, like a lot of the houses did. The first one, thinner, more fragile than the main door, had blown open and was somehow jammed in place. The second door appeared to be slightly, very slightly ajar. Sasha, the door expert, approached and inspected.

Ava, impatient as always, began scratching at the threshold. Sasha had told her many times that this wouldn't do any good, this time she saved her breath and continued her inspection as Ava continued her scratching. This door seemed a likely candidate for the push method.

She stood on her hind legs and put her paws on the door, it began to slowly open. Then, Sasha felt another force pushing against the door and it went back to its original position. The process repeated and she sat back down. Then, through the door, they heard a meow.

Although the meow didn't seem friendly, it wasn't a growl, so the cats decided to proceed. Sasha told the animal inside to sit back and wait, they could open the door but only if the cat wasn't pushing against it from the inside. Obviously, thought Sasha, this cat knew nothing about doors.

At this moment she recalled a story that one of their people used to tell. He'd joke about the indepth process he'd went through to gain admission to the tech school he attended after high school. If you could figure out whether the front door was push or pull, you could get in, then he would laugh laugh laugh. Sasha, not comprehending the joke, did understand the push versus pull issue. This door was obviously a push. Sasha questioned why this was such a difficult concept.

But it was. Sasha pushed and pushed and the door slowly gave way. Ava sat and watched, perplexed by what was going on. Sasha had tried to get Ava to help, with her added bulk it would be much easier pushing doors open, but she was steadfast in her resistance. Unable to grasp the concept she'd either sit down and watch the show, as she was doing now, or wander off, bored with the proceedings.

Eventually Sasha overcame whatever had been holding up the door and it swung wide open. Inside, they were greeted by a orange tiger kitty with pale yellowish green eyes. The cat was crouched low, ears back, fur up, hissing menacingly at the two invaders.

This is the thanks we get, thought Sasha. She told the cat that they didn't mean any harm, they were just opening the door. The cat gave a final hiss then sprung right between Sasha and Ava, jumped over a porch railing, and took off running through the yard, across the street and disappeared around a neighbor's house.

Sasha and Ava looked at each other, wow, wth. This had been the way with all the cats they'd met, none wanted anything to do with them. This one they'd rescued could have at least acknowledged their existence and thanked them.

The orange cat was long gone, they expected they'd never see it again. Dawn was still a long way off so, since they'd gone through all this trouble, the cats decided to explore the house. They walked inside not expecting to find a healthy rodent population in a house with a cat trapped inside.

They found the house in relatively good shape, dusty with a hint of a moldy smell in the air. The moldy smell was nearly overpowered by the strong smell of cat waste. They heard a few rodents but they were inside the walls. Here and there they found where the cat had dug and scratched at the base of these walls. They imagined it must have been very frustrating, hungry with a meal taunting you from the other side of a wall. The cats began to feel sorry for the orange tiger kitty and forgave him his poor manners.

They explored the house thoroughly as exploring was great fun for a cat. Upstairs they found piles of cat poo with small bones noticeable here and there. So not all the rodents were in the walls, they began to feel less sorry for their orange friend.

Many people pictures were on the walls and most flat surfaces had more. There were a few of an older lady holding an orange cat, or snuggling with the same cat in her lap. Both the lady and the cat looked extremely content. Seeing these only made Sasha and Ava miss their people more. They were back to feeling sorry for the orange tabby.

Sasha figured it was probably just the lady that lived here, with her cat. They were each other's best friends, going through this life together. And now they were separated, like so many other pets from their people. It was all so very sad.

Letting go of these sorrowful thoughts the cats continued to explore. They went downstairs to check out the basement. They found that it was a walkout, with a great big glass slider door. The door was completely uncovered and provided a massive view of the back yard. This must have been of further torment to the orange cat, wonderful full view of the outside but no possible way to get through such a sturdy slider. Sure enough, just as Sasha was thinking this, she noticed many scratch marks at the base of the door, the carpet had even been slightly shredded where it met the door frame. That poor cat.

Further explorations of the basement revelled two overflowing, and very disgusting, litter boxes, but the real find was two bags of cat food.

The bags weren't very big and had been positively shredded by the previous tenant but the cats were still able to find a small meal hidden in the recesses of the bags and scattered about on the floor. It was different food then what was in the bag back home and had a good taste, the cats ate all they could find. It can be hard for cat bellies to change so quickly to different foods. Later, because of this, there would be two upset little cat tummies. Both cats seemed to realized this but the food was good and they couldn't stop themselves.

When Sasha noticed a very slight light at the eastern horizon the cats decided to head for home. They had explored this house thoroughly. They had found many neglected cat toys along with several cat beds and trees. This evidence along with all the pictures convinced the cats that this had been a true cat lover's home, the older lady must have positively doted on the orange cat. The more they saw of all of this the more homesick Sasha and Ava became.

Eagerly they made their way home, each of them secretly hoping that they'd find that their people had returned. They both knew this wasn't likely but hope sometimes was all you had to keep you going.

They got home just as dawn was breaking, and, of course, there were no people. But there was plenty that was familiar, it was still their forever home. They snuggled up together in a favorite chair and went to sleep, dreaming of warm laps and chasing cat toys pulled by people.

Chapter 6

Lately the fleas, nasty little biting creatures, were beginning to take their toll. Sasha was tolerating it okay but Ava was a mess. She had dug at herself until she was bald and bleeding in several areas. Sasha had implored her to stop digging so feverishly as you can't dislodge the pesky little bugs and the constant scratching would only make it worse. But Ava couldn't seem to help herself and kept right on digging at her tattered flesh.

It was the rodents, both of the cats knew this. With the rodents came the fleas. There was no way around it, the cats couldn't live without the rodent supermarket that the houses had become.

Sasha supposed that with every silver lining there comes a dark cloud. She giggled slightly at the reversal of words, remembering her people and how she'd heard the man say that a few times. He was somewhat of a pessimist, and although he'd look for the silver lining whenever a dark cloud appeared he'd also be wary of a dark cloud that possibly might be following any silver lining he'd found. It was a humorous little game from Sasha's perspective.

Sitting there, thinking about her people, the silly things they would say, and watching poor Ava dig herself slowly to death, Sasha suddenly had an important memory pop into her little brain. She remembered her people talking, the man telling the little girl a story. It was about a fox that was having trouble with fleas and how he dealt with them. The man had read the story once, a long time ago. He couldn't remember where or when and didn't know if it was fact of fiction, only that it was an interesting story. The cats would have to risk another trip to the creek but it would be worth it, if her plan worked. If it didn't work at least the cold waters would help sooth Ava's burning skin.

Sasha convinced Ava to come to the creek with her. She didn't need much convincing once Sasha told her the reason for the trip. They went outside and were immediately greeted by a loud squawk from one of their blue jay friends. They exchanged greetings and chatted about the crisp weather. It was quite cold, and there was a thick frost on the ground. Sasha thought that this was perfect timing, the cold would put a damper on the flea population. But wow was that water going to be chilly.

Sasha told Mr. Blue Jay they were heading to the creek. The bird told them not to fear the dog pack, they were last spotted way to the west of their range, as far west as the birds had seen them. He even offered to be their lookout. Both cats thanked him. Sasha wondered if they would have ever survived without the surprising friendship with the area's many birds. Probably not. In turn the cats hunted only rodents. It wasn't much of a trade off. Rodents were easy, there was no need to hunt birds.

The cats cautiously made their way to the creek. They didn't want to be out during the day but this wasn't something they could do at night. Sasha's little head darted this way and that, searching for any threats. They trusted their blue jay friend but Sasha could not help herself, she'd had too many bad experiences to let down her guard, even a little. She especially didn't like being out in the daytime. The sun was shining, this made it even worse for her. Although, she thought, a nice warm sun on their backs might be a good thing once they left the creek.

They made their way along the fence row they'd followed before. It was in even worse shape but gave them some cover and cats don't really care about fences being painted and planks all in order.

They made a quick stop at the pond, hoping to say hi to the fish, only to find it completely frozen over. They had visited their fish friend a couple of times since their initial visit. The fish was, in its own way, very happy to see them, but still couldn't understand the person/people paradox. Too dimwitted for the cats' taste they didn't come to visit the fish very often, but feeling a little sorry for it they tried to stop in when they could. Besides, Sasha thought, if you listen closely enough you can learn something, even from the dumbest creature on earth.

Down by the pond they found the ice cloudy and covered with a buildup of crunchy snow. Sometimes, when it was a little windy and snowing, ice would form like this. They were unable to see through the ice so they moved on.

They angled away from the pond back towards the fence that they would follow towards the creek. They came across a pile of brush and broken tree branches, the result of the human that used to live here and his attempts to clean up the yard. Ava, being Ava, was much too curious to pass by a lovely pile of yard waste without performing a thorough investigation. She stepped up on a branch and poked her little head into the darkness to have a look.

Sasha, being Sasha, was becoming nervous and impatient and had already asked her sister more then once to leave the dirty pile of sticks and to please remember the reason they were out there. Ava stepped further into the pile, ignoring Sasha completely. Just then the blue jay squawked from a nearby tree. Sasha looked up at him in great alarm.

Mr Blue Jay, seeing her startled expression, quickly reassured her that all was okay and he'd only wanted to see what they were up to. He apologized for the loud squawk and said that he was a Blue Jay and that's what we do. Sasha noticed he was chuckling through much of his little speech. She didn't quite believe that the loud call was just an accident.

Sasha told the Blue Jay that Ava just had to investigate this pile of sticks and they might be here for a little while. The Blue Jay took off, calling to Sasha that all was clear and he would squawk many times if there really was a problem. Sasha turned her attention back to her sister whom had mostly disappeared into the depths of the pile. She reluctantly followed. She quickly caught up with Ava and found her calmly sitting and having a relaxing chat with her newest friend.

A cute bunny sat on the ground, deeper in the pile, but only a couple feet from Ava, twitching her little nose and watching the cats with mild interest. Ava was asking what the bunny was doing here and if this was her home. The bunny didn't answer, asking Ava what she was doing here. Ava replied that she was exploring because it was her favorite thing to do. To which the bunny replied that you are exploring in my home. Ava expressed regret for the disturbance but didn't leave, of course. The bunny sighed. That was what Sasha heard as she approached. The entire conversation, being held in animal speak, happened quite quickly.

Greetings being over the bunny invited the cats to stay for awhile, she had so few visitors nowadays. Now they could all relax and have a real chat. The cats told her that they came from the homes on the other side of the pond, way at the end of the fence row. The bunny knew of the houses but didn't like to go near them, she expressed a great fear of the people that lived there. The cats explained the people were gone and, if she wanted, she could come by for a visit. She twitched her nose a little at this, an interesting concept, visit a house.

She had suspected the people were gone, the world had changed so. There was little noise anymore and the air smelled so clean, like she always thought it should smell. But visit a house? She apologized and said this was too much for her, she couldn't see herself in a house. They told her that if she ever changed her mind she should come looking for them.

They all talked about the dogs and the howling of coyotes and how it made them all very nervous. They covered the subject of the missing people thoroughly but came to no conclusions as to what may have happened to them. They spoke about homes and what that meant, something very different to each of them. The bunny said she was going to spend the winter here in her brush pile and hoped she'd be safe. The cats figured the houses would be safer but who knew for sure?

All in all it was a very nice visit and the cats made another friend. Eventually they had to go, they were heading to the creek and wanted to take care of their business while the sun was still high in the sky. The bunny didn't ask why they were going to the creek, only asking them to stop by again sometime for another visit. She was glad they came by and said she really enjoyed their talk. The cats said goodbye and headed off towards the creek.

Once at the creek Sasha explained her plan and told Ava she'd go first to show her how it was done. They had to search a bit to find a likely spot as there was some ice on the creek. Luckily the flowing water had kept it from freezing completely over.

Once they'd decided on a spot there was no holding Ava back, so anxious she was to rid herself of the horrible, biting pests. She understood the concept and was going first, whether Sasha liked it or not. Sasha told her to go slow and be patient as this wouldn't work otherwise. Ava found a small twig, grasped it tightly in her mouth, and began to wade slowly into the creek. To Sasha's surprise Ava looked like she was going to follow her advice.

The creek was definitely cold as Ava took her first tentative steps into the clear water. She slowly waded in until her four paws were all submersed, then she paused and looked back at Sasha. Ava was desperate and wanted Sasha's plan to work, she was determined to follow Sasha's instructions as best she could. Ava knew her dear friend was the wiser of the two and appreciated her for it.

Sasha nodded at Ava, told her she was doing fine, and encouraged her to wade a little deeper. Ava took another couple steps and paused, half of each leg was submerged. She again looked back at Sasha who told her to slowly step further into the stream until the water reached her belly. As she did this she thought she could feel little creatures scurrying up her legs and onto her belly. She didn't know if she was imagining this but hoped she wasn't.

Sasha told her she was doing perfect and to keep slowly wading further out. As the water deepened she began to shiver but this she hardly noticed. After another minute or so her entire body was underwater. She'd held her tail down so that it was the first to submerge. She now knew for sure that Sasha's plan was working as she'd felt many of the terrible little fleas migrating up her body to her head, now the only dry place.

Cats being cats neither of them liked the idea of being in the water but Ava hardly noticed her distaste for the current situation. Her head was covered in very active fleas and it was all she could do to contain her excitement and continue to slowly execute Sasha's plan. She went further out and tilted her head upward. Soon only her short snout and the stick she tightly held were above the waterline.

Water was getting in her eyes and mouth, she held her breath. She resisted the urge to clamp her eyes shut when they went below the water's surface, her amazement at what was unfolding before them gave her the strength to keep them open. Hundreds of fleas were jumping and crawling, scurrying and walking, out onto the twig she carried in her mouth.

Now only the twig and the very tip of her snout were above the water. Her eyes crossed and she could have sworn that she saw one last flea, there on her nose, look back at her and shake his little fist in defiance before turning and jumping onto the twig. Then Ava submersed totally, letting go of the twig at the same time. What a sight she must have been, a cat totally underwater, eyes open wide as she watched her tormentors float away.

Sasha repeated the process to perfection. She had to admit that watching Ava execute the plan so precisely motivated her to do the same. Being in the water was a terrible thing to these two cats and Sasha wasn't so sure she'd have done as well if she'd gone first. Ava seemed to stand a little taller, a little prouder, when she told her this. It was a good day for Ava, the first in a long time.

They shook themselves silly trying to dry off as best they could. The sun was still shining and felt good warming them as they made their way back home. Thanking the Blue Jay, they went inside. The cats found that they could dry themselves off somewhat by rolling around on a rug, then, even better, on a bed.

They squirmed under blankets and rolled back and forth on sheets, playing and laughing. Once they felt a little dryer they cuddled together on the floor by a window where the sun was streaming in. They groomed themselves and soon they slept. It had been a long time, especially for Ava, since she'd slept so soundly, not interrupted by biting little bugs.

It was dark out when the cats awoke, shivering and hungry. The adventure at the creek the day before had been exhausting. They had been cold and wet for a long time, but they had slept well, something that had been impossible for Ava with the flea problem. Ava, especially was excited and didn't mind the cold and hunger all that much. She was practically smiling! For some reason the fleas had been extra hard on her and she was just ecstatic to be rid of them and feel this good.

They were both quite hungry and decided to get a small snack at the food bag before heading out to hunt. The bag had little left inside, they had to crawl all the way in to eat. They realized this was a problem but couldn't help themselves. They wanted to save some food for the winter but the adventure at the creek had taken a lot out of them. They needed to refuel before they could do anything.

After eating they went outside to investigate and find a place to hunt. A cloud cover had moved in and even with the sun down, it didn't feel as cold out as it had earlier in the day. There was a puddle in the front drive with a thin layer of ice. Ava stepped on the ice and crunched through to the cool water. They drank deeply, both of them enjoying the clean water. Without people and cars zooming around it seemed that every puddle was the cleanest, freshest water they had ever drank. Amazing how something as simple as a drink of cold, clean water could be so appreciated.

Being worn out from the day before neither of them were in a mood for a big adventure, maybe a first for Ava. They decided to hunt the first house they'd been able to access since the people left. This was the house where a big branch had crashed through a window making a natural bridge to the inside.

They'd been saving this house for later, when the snows came, and they needed a place nearby to hunt. The house, having not been hunted since the early days, was positively overrun with rodents. They were caught by surprised and not used to being hunted, the cats made quick work of them.

It was still early into the night and the cats, with bellies full, decided to poke around the house a little more before going home. There wasn't much to see, just another house smelling of rodent urine, dusty and wet.

In the basement they found nearly a pond. The water was everywhere, but only a couple inches deep. This was much too deep for the cats. After their adventures at the creek they wanted nothing to do with getting wet.

Back upstairs they went to exploring the kitchen. There were packages scattered about, cupboard doors open, and just a general mess. They were surprised that rodents could make such a mess. Looking about at all the debris they found nothing that a cat would like to eat. In fact, after inspecting a little more closely, Sasha noticed that a lot of the old food boxes and packages, already torn open and looted, were mostly empty. It began to dawn on her that this many rodents couldn't sustain themselves forever in a home where no one was bringing more food to restock the pantry.

She decided to explore the kitchen a little more thoroughly, maybe confirm her suspicions that the mice were quickly going through the food supply.

Using her superior door opening skills she was able to open the door of a tall cabinet. Inside she found many undisturbed can goods on higher shelves. The boxes were all opened, although there was sugar and flour packages that still had a good amount left. Pasta boxes were emptied, it appeared they'd gone first.

She opened a cupboard containing pots and pans, another with bowls and other cookware. Then she opened a third and was greeted with a dull and sluggish hullo.

What looked like the biggest rat she'd ever seen peered out, blinking its eyes. Sasha squatted low, put back her ears, puffed up, and hissed at the creature. Ava walked over and curiously looked in the cabinet, doing none of these things.

The creature spoke to them again, in familier animal speak, and asked them to leave him alone, he just wanted to sleep here and not be disturbed. He'd just gotten used to the scurrying of all these pesky mice and now cats come along, what a bother.

Sasha said nothing, still in a defensive stance. The creature looked at her and chuckled. His laugh told her to just relax, he wasn't moving from this spot for the next several months, if he could help it.

The chuckle had been friendly enough. Sasha's fur settled slightly and she stopped hissing, but she remained crouched with her ears back.

Through all this Ava sat beside her sister, totally at ease, sitting as if she hadn't a care in the world. She looked at this new creature with wide staring eyes. The creature surprised Ava by speaking directly to her. It had noticed her gaping look and grumpily asked what Ava was staring at. After a moment Ava gathered herself and asked the creature if it weren't the king of all the mice.

The creature stared blankly at Ava, seeing how disarming she was in her wonder, and began to chuckle. Soon he was laughing, his eyes squinting, tears at the corners. Sasha was now sitting by her sister, wonder and surprise in her eyes too, the fear all but gone.

Eventually he stopped chuckling and got control of himself. He answered the cats, telling them that no, he was not the king of mice, (chuckling again as he said it), he was a possum and this was where he'd chosen to winter.

Ava asked what that meant and that brought on an entire conversation concerning hibernating. She didn't quite grasp this, it would probably come up later in the winter.

The possum turned a little to face the cats, made himself comfortable, and they continued to talk.

Amongst the wild animals the big topic of conversation, as it was with the former pets, was whatever happened to the people. For the most part the wild animals all agreed - good riddance. Their homes made great dens, their roads were now much safer, and the food they left behind was a delight. At one point the possum asked if the cats knew whether or not the people would be coming back. By choosing to winter in a house this was, of course, a great concern of the possum. The cats told him they had no idea, to which he seemed to find comfort and relief. This was the opposite of how the cats felt.

They spoke about the other animals, both wild and former pets. The possum cautioned them saying that, if they continued to frequent strange houses, they'd likely run into other wild animals wintering there. They spoke about the dogs, everyone was getting more and more concerned about them. One dog wasn't that hard to deal with, but they were forming packs and that made the possum and his wild friends nervous. That, the possum said, was the main reason he'd chosen this house to winter in. The only access was by crawling along the branch that had fallen through the window. The branch wasn't big enough for most dogs, and they'd likely injure themselves on the jagged shards remaining in the window frame if they tried to get in. He felt reasonably safe here and figured he'd get a good winter's sleep, that is if he wasn't constantly disturbed by curious cats. This last he said with a smile and a wink. The cats smiled in return. People would never notice these kind of smiles, they came from the eyes.

After they'd spoken for a really long time, much longer than anyone would ever think a possum and a couple of cats would speak, the cats decided it was time to go home. They told the possum good night and thanked him very much for his warnings and safety advice. It was valuable information for the former pets, wild animals knew what it took to survive and the cats knew they could learn much from them. And, they figured, it wouldn't be very often that one would take the time to speak with them at all.

As they left they apologized for waking the possum and told him they wouldn't wake him again. The possum chuckled and said it was okay, he was glad for the conversation and it didn't hurt him one bit to wake up for a little while. He'd be waking on occasion throughout the winter. Before they left he did ask them for a favor, that if they saw people coming around that they'd please come and wake him. Smiling, he promised he wouldn't be mad.

The cats returned his smile and promised they'd come wake him if people came around, or if any other danger threatened. Then they snuck over the window sill and out into the cold world, making their way quickly back to their forever home.

The possum curled up in a tight little ball and quickly fell back asleep, a sounder slumber then before, as he was quite comforted to know that he'd made two new friends, friends that had his back.

Chapter 7

For the next couple of weeks the cats continued on in this way. As before, to avoid dogs and other creatures that might harm them, they were only hunting at night. They were getting rather good at this. They had preserved some of their food, not much, but good for an emergency.

This day they awoke late in the afternoon but it was still too early to go hunting so they sat in their favorite chair and watched the world through the window. As the sun began to set Ava wanted to go exploring, she still had that desire for adventure and was tired of hunting rodents in the same old houses. She was becoming impatient for the sun to set. Sasha reminded her of the dog pack they'd seen roaming around and they needed to be sure it was dark before they went out. It was obvious the leader was the tan and white dog, TW for short, the dog they had met at the creek and narrowly escaped. There were several dogs and it was best this group was avoided.

This evening the cats thought they would explore across the road. What was once a very busy and frightening passage was now eerily quiet. There was no traffic, just a wide expanse of asphalt. They approached the road cautiously as they couldn't quite let go of their fear, even though there were no longer any cars.

The cats stopped just a few feet from the road and hid behind a small evergreen bush. The sun had set, something the cats welcomed. A comforting blanket of darkness enveloping the cats, their superior night vision giving them an advantage over many other creatures. They looked and listened and were amazed, not for the first time, at the deathly quiet.

They spoke quietly about days long gone when they used to sit in the sun room and watch the traffic zip by. If they were lucky one of their people would open a window and they would sit and sniff at the gentle summer breeze, breathing deep the sweet fresh air. It was one of their favorite past times, watching and listening to the noises of the road, scooting down and peering over the window ledge when a dog would go by on the sidewalk. They weren't really afraid of the dogs, they were always pulling one of their people along by a short rope they had tied to their persons hand. The dogs' wouldn't be able to run fast, but caution was in a cats' nature.

After they were done reminiscing they crept out from behind the bush and out onto the pavement. It was damp but almost warm, the slight amounts of snow had melted only sticking around the edges and under trees here and there. It was a cold evening but it had been a sunny day, the road felt like the sun was still shining but only on the pads of their little feet.

Slowly they went, their bellies nearly brushing the pavement. Sasha had been cautious from the very first time they went outside, but Ava had learned her lesson and was now nearly as cautious as Sasha. Both cats were on high alert, they were very exposed out in the middle of the road. They looked this way and that, stopping every few steps to sniff at the air and listen intently. About half way they both broke into a run and scampered quickly across the remainder of the road, tired of the tension of being so far out in the open.

On the other side was an old abandoned farmhouse. Only a few short months ago it had been an active place with people coming and going, like any other home. But now it sat quiet and dark. The cats hid in a small bush near the front porch and closely examined their surroundings.

From their sun room they could look out across the road and see this stately old farmhouse. The mature trees and old bushes, many out buildings and barns, and a fenced in pasture where, from time to time, cows would wander into their field of vision.

It was only this past summer that there had been calfs. These little cows were fun to watch, they played often, like all children do. They would scamper about, kicking out with their back legs, and chase each other for no apparent purpose. Watching them you could feel the exhilaration for life that was typically reserved for the very young, and sometimes for the young at heart.

Sasha mentioned that they should see if the house was open so they left their hiding place and made their way to the front porch. They approached the front steps, Ava in the lead as she typically was, not being quite as cautious as Sasha. Ava no more then placed a paw on the first step when both cats froze, severely shocked by a sound they'd just heard. The sound had been simply a kind and pleasant 'good evening' but, as we all know, even the routine can be shocking when unexpected.

At the top of the steps, several feet to the right of the front door, sat a rough looking tomcat on and old wicker chair. He was well hidden in the darkness, which seemed very thick in the depths of the porch. The cats were still, looking each other over, not sure what to do. Sasha had pinned her ears back and raised her hackles, Ava appeared unafraid and rather curious of the entire situation. Sasha noted the ripped screen on the front door and gathered that the farm cat used this entrance to gain access to the house.

The cat followed her gaze and confirmed that this was indeed his home. He spoke slowly and gently, and was quite relaxed. Listening to him you'd think he was, as he talked, smiling a pleasant grandfatherly smile, that is, if cats could smile. He told Sasha that she had nothing to fear and he was glad that both cats had decided to stop by for a visit. Sasha began to relax and all three cats sat on the porch and got to know each other.

They had seen him before, as they sat in the sun room and watched the activity at the farm. And he had seen them as they sat watching out the windows. He told of how he'd always lived here at this farm but had never been in the house, that is until the people were gone, now he spent a good deal of time inside.

The people that lived here mostly ignored him but they were always kind and never cruel. They gave him cow milk and there was always a water bowl to drink from in the barn. The food bowl often ran empty but he was very appreciative when they would fill it. He would hunt around the farm to tide him over, figuring that maybe that's what the farmers expected of him.

Sasha and Ava made a little silly and asked him his name at nearly the same time. If you'd of been listening you'd have thought for sure all three cats were smiling now. It was good to have friends, very good indeed, and it seemed they had one more. The older cat, but not too old, maybe just a little older than the girls, said he was never given a name. But he recalled his early days, while still with his mother and her small litter of kittens. He had been the only male and it seemed he was just getting to know his mother and siblings when the farmer and his little girl had happened across them.

Before this, people had been coming and going and two of his sisters were taken. It was very strange, he felt sad and happy at the same time. They were going to their forever homes. His mother tried to comfort him and explain that lucky little kittens get adopted by people and then went to live happy lives with them. Shortly after this he had been scooped up by the farmers' little girl. He was excited and scared and he looked back at his mother and mewed. She told him she loved him and to be brave and, with a little tear glistening in her eye, she said 'goodbye my little prince, have a wonderful life'.

Sasha and Ava, touched by his story, would call him Prince from then on. He smiled at this, in the way that cats smile, hidden from the outside world, and said he liked being called Prince.

Why did he live outside when his people were there, Sasha and Ava wondered. He said that the farmer wouldn't have animals in the house. The little girl pitched a heck of a good fit but it was of no use.

The girl spent a great deal of time with him when they were both young. But, as time went by and she grew up, well, for a young lady there were many more important things to do then hang around with a mangy old cat.

The girls could tell he was sad about this, but it was the kind of sadness that was a part of life, and it made you smile a little bit inside when you think about it. Life is just that way, it's not always a story book or a fairy tale, but if you look at it long enough there's always something good to see. If you can understand that you can understand why he was never angry with the little girl, she just grew up and went her own way. She would still greet him every day with a sweet 'hello kitty kat, how are you?', and a quick pet, but the days of spending real time together were childhood memories. He would smile to himself and think of those days as he watched her walk away. He still loved his little girl and wondered where she was now and hoped she was okay.

Ava had asked Prince why they had never given him a name. He was never sure, she always called him kitty kat, but never a true name. Maybe it was because the farmer would never let an animal become a part of the family. Nothing against the farmer he'd went on to say, that was just how the farmer was and how he'd been brought up to be. Caretaker to the animals, but not emotionally attached.

He was a good caretaker, never cruel and always kind and that said more about a person then words ever could. Sasha and Ava both admired and were puzzled by Prince's kindness towards the farmer. It must have been a harsh life. Prince said it had been nothing but a good life, the best of lives, and that he was truly blessed. The cats sat in silence for a few minutes, lost in thought, remembering the good lives they shared with their people. It was a hard lesson to learn, but a very important one, seeing through the bad and finding the good.

They sat and chatted late into the night. They spoke fondly of their people and the crazy, silly things they would do. They laughed about the irony of humans, so strong it seemed to be a part of their very soul. How they were constantly on a never ending quest to acquire more and more things to make their lives easier, funner, happier, fuller, but were so stressed out in the pursuit and care of all these things that they made their lives anything but easier, funner, happier, fuller. All three of the cats could recall many times that they would sit and unemotionally watch people rush about, fretting about this and that, never happy, never content. They just wanted to give them a good slap and say settle down, if you are warm and your belly is full you've got more then you deserve. Take a break, sit with me and look out of the window and let life fill you up instead of spending all your time chasing what you hope would fill you. Yes, their people were odd creatures, they all agreed on this. So smart but so infinitely stupid at the same time. How could they survive without the cats presence to calm them down. The cats worried about their people, for the first time they were off on their own. They hoped the people would be okay.

They talked about how life had been since the people left. Prince said he'd taken to hunting only at night and had learned to be wary of other animals that may trespass on the farm. Sasha and Ava mentioned the run in they'd had with the mean dog down by the creek but they'd also learned that not all animals were to be feared. They told the story of Clarence, the robin Sasha had befriended that lonely night so long ago. They mentioned the strange antics of their squirrel friend. They told of the meetings they'd had with the possum, fish and bunny. Prince agreed that not all creatures were to be feared and was amazed that the girls had made so many friends. He especially enjoyed the story about the robin and hoped that he'd get to meet him someday.

They spoke of many fond memories and of how life wasn't the same without their people. As they spoke they were filled with happiness and were content. Good feelings flooded out into the deep darkness of the porch that night. It was good to have friends. The cats went back home with promises of another visit the next night.

Over the next few days the cats' friendship grew. They spent the early evenings hanging out on the porch of the old farmhouse, telling stories and chatting about how things used to be. The nights they would hunt, both around the farm and across the road in the rodent infested houses. They still slept at their separate homes but other then that spent most of their time together.

These three cats had formed their own little pack, a quite uncommon thing among cats. Times had changed and they needed to do what they had to do to survive, and their small pack might just be the edge they needed. The dogs were forming packs and the worst of them had TW at the head, the dog from the incident at the creek.

This night had brought a fine dusting of snow adding to what was already on the ground. They were turning the corner towards winter. This thought frightened Sasha as she had been cold before. They had spoken about the coming cold of winter on one of their late afternoon front porch chatting sessions. Prince seemed unconcerned and said they would manage just fine. Sasha had her doubts. Ava had a slight inclination that being cold and fighting through deep snow might be difficult but her only experience with winter was laying on a comfortable chair, warm and fed, watching the snowfall outside.

Chapter 8

It had been a difficult night hunting and they'd noticed the first rays of the morning sun before they decided to call it. Prince bid them good day and headed back to his farm. Sasha and Ava were tired and looking forward to a long morning nap. Slowly the cats made their way across the neighbors yard, home in sight. As they walked a thin layer of snow chilled their feet. A cardinal swooped down, chirping at the cats. Clarence had gone south for the winter but the cats still had a few friends in the sky and this cardinal was one.

He nervously tweeted to the cats, the cats quickly understood, TW's pack was near. They started to run towards home but the bird tweeted louder, grabbing the cats attention and bringing them to a stop. No, the bird had said, the dogs are over by your house. The cats backed away and soon saw the dogs coming towards them.

Up ahead the cats saw the dogs come around a corner. In a couple seconds TW saw them and, with hardly a pause, the chase was on. Luckily the bird had sounded the alarm while they were still near trees, a minute later and the dogs would have found them on open ground, and the cats would have had no hope. With the dogs nearly upon them they were just able to climb to safety. It would be a long day.

TW and the other dogs taunted the cats and circled the base of the tree. Come down, we'll make it quick, TW had said. The hours passed by slowly, giving the cats plenty of time to observe their tormentors.

There were six dogs. TW was the obvious leader. Next in the pecking order seemed to be a sleek gray shepherd mix, circling the tree and looking at the cats with unnervingly intelligent eyes. He was called Shep.

All the dogs went by their 'pack' name, their old names given by their lost families never used.

Shep was a beautiful dog, with light blue eyes and some gray fur mixed in with the black and browns of a traditional shepherd. He was sleek, maybe a little smaller than a pure breed, but faster. He had the same strong and long snout. When he looked at you, you could feel the intelligence.

He'd been adopted by a family with two teenagers, both of whom had gone off to college after he'd lived there just a couple years. He'd been brought home as just a puppy and, although he was loved well enough, he got the feeling that he was replacing someone, a previous family member. As he got older, and a little wiser, he was sure of it.

He'd seen many pictures around the house of the four people and a shaggy black dog with curly hair and floppy ears. The family looked so happy in these pictures. The early pictures showed this dog with two little kids, the later showed the same dog, only it was very old and the kids were as they were when Shep had moved it. The pictures told the story.

After the kids had moved out the older couple were friendly enough but they didn't play with him and hardly ever took him for walks. Begrudgingly they'd take him out on a short leash to do his business. This was terribly embarrassing. He'd lay in the TV room with them while they watched their shows. He'd watch them leave in the mornings and then sit and look out the window, waiting patiently for their return. He would often sigh deeply. Slowly he grew sad and despondent.

One day, in a rush, the older couple just left. They'd put him in the fenced in backyard, ran around gathering this and that, obviously very agitated, then got in the family car and took off. He couldn't see the car from the backyard but he knew its sound well enough. He listened to it until the sound faded into the distance. He remembered that day well, he always would. Sitting down in the back yard, a slight rain falling, straining his ears, listening for the sound of the car to return, waiting, waiting, waiting.

It got dark, still he waited. The dawn broke, he paced the yard, waiting. They hadn't left him any food or water. As that first day wore on he became very thirsty. He licked at the wet grass, still damp from the day before. Soon the sun took even that from him.

Eventually he decided to leave and quickly dug under the fence and was gone. Maybe, if he'd been more attached to these people, and they to him, he'd have waited more than a day. Maybe, if he had waited more than a day, he would have been too thirsty, too hungry, too tired, to fend for himself, and he wouldn't be here now. Life was full of maybes.

Next there was a black terrier mutt the other dogs had nicknamed Rat. He was maybe 25 pounds, small and compact, and with a vicious bark. He was spending his time barking at the cats and jumping and biting at the lower branches.

Rat had been loved by his forever family but he was a terribly unpopular dog in his neighborhood. He had gotten into fights with other dogs and had even bitten a neighbor once. For this he was severely scolded. The scolding didn't frighten him. What did was the tones his people used as he overheard them discussing the incident. It sounded ominous, he actually feared for his life, and, what made it worse is he didn't know why.

In his opinion the neighbor had deserved it. He had strolled right up to the woman that Rat thought of as his pack leader, with his hand outstretched and his teeth bared. How was he to know that the man was reaching to shake his pack leaders hand in a sign of greeting, and smiling to show he was happy to see her.

He'd come from behind, taken hold of the man's calf, and given a mighty shake. The taste of blood and resulting screams were very satisfying. Needless to say the man instantly backed off of his pack leader.

That night was the night he heard his people, in hushed and dark tones, discussing his fate. He'd only done what he thought was right, why was he in trouble? He'd never understand people. It was only a couple of nights after this that his people had been taken by rough looking men in uniforms. He'd given chase but one of them kicked him hard in the head, sending him crashing into the wall. When he regained consciousness the house was dark and the front door was wide open.

He went outside, the cool night air relieving some of the pain in his head. There were no signs of his people. Their scent ended somewhere in the driveway, like it often did, like they just disappeared into thin air.

He waited there for his people, waited in the driveway. He slept there. The next day he roamed around outside the house, found some standing water to drink, but ended up coming back to the driveway. That night he again spent sleeping in the driveway, waiting. Sometime towards morning, when it was still dark, it got too cold for him and he went inside and slept on his doggy bed.

The following day he'd held vigil in the driveway for a few more hours until a German short hair came trotting by. The dog stopped and beckoned him. Normally he'd have torn after this strange dog like a bat out of hell but, well, there was no one here anymore and he'd lost his desire to guard, well, nothing.

So he'd went with this dog. They ran together for a couple of days, eating whatever they could find, drinking from mud puddles. Then they just split up. The other dog wanted to head down a road for no particular reason. Rat had wanted a reason and just sat down. He watched stubbornly as the other dog trotted off. Eventually he'd hooked up with TW and found a place in his pack. Like Shep, he'd pretty much moved on from his forever home, hardly ever reminiscing.

It was different for Goldie, a golden retriever. He looked to be a beautiful dog but the time in the wild had played havoc with his coat. He was more mild mannered and seemed to be doing mostly what was expected of him, circling the tree and letting out an occasional nervous bark.

He'd been adopted into a great forever home with four great kids and loving parents. They played with him constantly, took him everywhere, and he had the run of the house. He slept in whatever person's bed he chose, the chosen one always excited to be picked. They kept him well fed and often indulged him with table scraps. His had truly been a wonderful life.

He'd pretty much blocked out how he'd ended up on his own, not even really sure how he got involved with this pack. TW had bullied him out of his sullen depression with numerous threats and generally rough treatment so he'd eventually learned to just do what was expected and he'd at least be left alone.

The next dog was a small fluffy white girl. The cats had seen many of her type before the people left. She looked like she might have been a nice girl at one time, a lap dog that loved her people. Now her white coat was very dirty and clotted and she barked constantly at the cats with what seemed to be a tremendous amount of effort.
Her barking was loud and high pitched and constant, more annoying than anything the other dogs could muster. The pack called her Fluff. She much preferred the name her people had given her, Bella, but never spoke of it. Sasha named her Jericho in her mind, her barking could truly bring down city walls.

Fluff had lived with a small family, including two half sized people and a grumpy old cat. As the kids grew older she was often ignored, but the lady of the house was always kind and loving. She would even take her out for short walks. It was a dependable, if boring, existence. Relatives, including their dogs, would sometimes visit, the only break in the monotony. Not that she ever complained, she was happy with her simple little life.

It had been hard at first, being on her own. She figured her people would come for her, but she'd ended up living on the street, homeless and sad. She wasn't really sure of any of this and it was all getting rather confused in her little mind.

She met up with an older black dog and they ran together for a while before they were brought to this pack by Goldie. The leader wasn't happy but eventually relented and let them join, the more the merrier.

Fluff looked familiar to the cats, they remembered her as being the standoffish little dog that was with the last member of the pack. That dog was the older black lab mix that was now sitting off to the side, looking lost and forlorn.

The pack called the black lab mix Slow. He was standing by himself off at the edge of the action. He was older than the other dogs and the years had slowed him down, this caused TW to give him the unflattering name. They recognized this dog, he was the one they'd met in the early days, soon after the people left. Fluff, of course, had been with Slow the last time they'd met. She hadn't liked the cats then either.

Slow sadly looked at the cats stuck in the tree and they met his gaze. They could tell he felt bad for them but there was nothing he could do. It appeared he was last in the packs' pecking order. He sat in the snow, watching.

Slow had a peaceful and happy life with his family in the before days. There was a woman and a man and two boys who were full grown now. Slow remembered coming home for the first time, the boys were much smaller then and they all took to him right away. They grew up together, those boys and him. It had been a great life. But it had all ended and all he was doing now was surviving.

Hope that he would see his family again had kept him going, but that hope was fading and so was he. In a kind of trance he followed the pack around, tolerating the bully TW as best he could, eating whatever scraps were left for him, surviving, hope fading.

For a long time the dogs circled the tree making life generally miserable for the cats. They would run off, one or two at a time, then come back. The day wore on. Some of them even napped under the tree, on the snowy ground. The one constant was the yipping of the small white dog. She was really, really getting on the cats nerves.

The morning passed. The afternoon was slipping by. Were these dogs going to stay here through the night? The thought made Sasha tremble. The cats heard a familiar chattering and looked up to see their friend Mr. Squirrel calling to them from a nearby tree. Oh my, this is trouble, this is trouble, trouble, trouble he'd said. But never fear, Mr Squirrel is here, or this is what he seemed to say with all his chattering and fidgeting about.

Animal speak could be different every time. Sometimes it would be silent, looks telling the story. Other times there would be the sounds that different animals make accompanied, or not, by movements depending on whether the animal thought them necessary to communicate. It could be very complex. Sasha figured that was probably why their humans had such a hard time understanding them. They would try so very hard but invariably get everything all mixed up. Despite the current situation Sasha smiled as she remembered the confused looks her people would give her as she tried to convey to them the simplest of things. The poor simple people, they tried so hard but just never were able to turn the corner when it came to true understanding, bless their little hearts.

The squirrel chattered some more, breaking Sasha's train of thought, and capturing the cats attention. He told the cats he wanted to help them and he had a plan. He loved tormenting dogs so this would be great fun.

He'd tormented many dogs through closed windows and doors and at the end of strong chains. Secretly he'd remembered tormenting a few cats, mostly through closed windows while hanging precariously from a bird feeder. He loved watching the cats jump and paw at the window while he munched away. He didn't mention this to the cats.

Putting past thoughts aside the squirrel began making a rustling in the trees as he jumped from branch to branch. The dogs noticed. The squirrel had become a master at taunting house pets and he put his talents on full display.

The squirrel came down to a low branch and called out to the dogs. In animal speak he was basically saying 'you can't get me'.

The squirrel continued to hop precariously about on low hanging branches, a tempting target for untrained dogs, not wise to the ways of treehoppers like this little guy. The taunting soon got under TW's skin, surprisingly thin for such a bully of a dog. TW told Slow to stay, then he and the rest of the pack took off after the squirrel. Never mind that this was one small squirrel, not even a meal for one dog, TW's pride was now at stake. They could so get the squirrel, he'd show him.

Directions were not given, Slow was just told to stay, so he stayed. The dogs all seemed to forget about the cats and were frantically going after the squirrel. The thrill of the chase taking them over completely.

Slow was gentle and kind and spoke with the cats in the tree with polite greetings. He said he was sorry about their predicament but he had a plan.

Soon the squirrel had led the other dogs quite far away. Slow told the cats that he hated TW and hated being part of the pack and he still missed his people terribly. He said he didn't know what would happen to him but no longer cared, he didn't want to see his friends hurt, so, with the other dogs far away, he told them to run. TW told him to stay, so that's what he planned to do.

There was something kind about this dog and the cats trusted him. Even Sasha, with her cautious nature, trusted the old dog, although she thought maybe they could outrun him anyway as he didn't seem to be in such great shape. He was terribly thin, much thinner then when they first met him.

So off went the cats to hide in a nearby house, not their own, and watch and listen. Eventually the other dogs returned, squirrel less.

TW, who was already quite angry because of the squirrel, became absolutely livid when he learned the cats were gone. He tormented and degraded Slow for losing the cats. The cats heard a loud yelp and, peeking out a window, saw Slow on his back and TW standing over him. Sasha and Ava felt sad and afraid for their friend but soon the pack headed out and Slow got up and followed. A close call again for the cats, saved by the most unlikely of cat friends, a bird, a squirrel, and a dog.

Chapter 9

The dogs traveled some time without speaking. TW was still glowering over the loss of the cats. Along with losing that damnable squirrel his pride had taken a double whammy today. Deep down he knew the cats wouldn't make much of a meal but it was personal now. They had embarrassed him at the creek and now eluded him again with more trickery. His anger was forming into determination. He would deal with the cats, he promised himself.

The other dogs followed TW in silence, trotting along the shoulder of the once busy main road, the same road that passed by the cats home. Evening was upon them and they were heading west. The sun, sitting low in the cloudless south western sky, gave them very little warmth. They all knew it would be a cold night, one of many to come. They were heading in the direction of the abandoned home they had taken over as their den.

Shep had crossed the road and was exploring the edges of a farmers field, alert for signs of danger or hopefully a meal. He kept pace with the pack and occasionally stopped to paw at the ground, investigating an interesting smell. This field had been planted with beans which Shep dined on as he trotted along. The pack had all become omnivores, the unharvested fields a main source of sustenance.

With a black muzzle, ears, sides and back and the rest of him a mixture of brown and grays and beautiful light blue eyes, he really was a striking dog. A shepherd mix, he had all the physical characteristics of a shepherd only not quite as tall and a little sleeker.

A very smart dog, he constantly questioned TW, pointing out alternate routes and different food sources. TW wasn't very bright but he was smart enough to value Shep's input, knowing they probably wouldn't survive the long winter without it.

The two stood about the same height but TW was a much stronger, thicker dog. There was no question who would win out in a physical altercation. In the human world a Shep would have a hundred TW's working for him, lifting and loading and doing other manual tasks for minimum wage. But here in the wild, living in a pack, brute strength would always win out. Unless, of course, Shep resorted to some kind of trickery, which he figured some day he would.

To his credit, Shep appreciated TW and his strength. The coyotes were beginning to crowd their territory and TW would be instrumental in their ability to survive a confrontation with these wild animals. Shep had seen the coyotes and figured they could deal with one or two, but any more than that, taking flight would be the wisest option.

Shep ran up to the road and saw Rat and Fluff in their usual position, scampering close behind TW, little legs pumping to keep up. These two had become inseparable, always together as the pack roamed, cuddling at night for warmth. It wasn't romantic, more of a buddy system that worked for them. They talked as they trotted, describing what they'd do once they finally caught the cats. Part of this was for TW's benefit as they were both always eager to say or do anything that would help them get on TW's good side.

Fluff wondered if TW had a good side. She knew he wasn't very bright but he was vicious and maybe that's all he was, there was no other 'side'. It didn't matter to her, she depended on the pack and he was the leader. She'd do what she had to to survive. She didn't much care for cats in general and never really wished them any harm, but if TW wanted them she'd chase and bark and do whatever was expected of her.

When she was just a pup and was brought to her forever home she had her only experience with cats by getting to know the grumpy old cat that already lived there. As a puppy everything was new and exciting and she always wanted to play, like puppies always do. She'd tried to make friends with the old cat but he'd scowl at her and run and hide. He told her many times he didn't want any friends and he most certainly did not want to play with a puppy.

After she'd lived with her people for about a year the old cat had started getting sickly and was having trouble using his litter box. The lady person treated him kindly enough but there was a sadness in her voice as she spoke to him, Bella could sense this well enough. (Fluff, unlike the other dogs, always used her people name when she thought about past times.)

As the old cat's condition worsened he would, from time to time, speak with Bella. Sometimes, when the sun was shining on the living room rug they'd sun themselves and talk about almost anything. Bella was no longer a puppy and had calmed down somewhat, and she realized the old cat would not tolerate much more then sitting in the sun and chatting. Bella enjoyed these relaxing times, memories of which often helped sustain her through the hard times she now had to endure.

The cat spoke to Bella about how he'd lived with the little family for a long time. He reminisced about the day he'd been chosen from the litter and had said goodbye to his mom and sisters and brothers.

He spoke about being disappointed when his people brought home the first wailing little infant. They must have gone a great distance to get the miniature human because they were gone for a couple days and nights.

He'd questioned why they had chosen such a noisy human when there surely must have been much quieter ones in the litter. This one wailed away the nights. He talked about how he'd tried to be friendly with the new little human but his people always shooed him away.

By the time the second infant came along he hardly felt like a part of the family anymore. As the little humans grew they would chase him when he didn't want to be chased, hold him when he didn't want to be held, and generally annoy the snot out of him. And so he'd become a little too grumpy and a little too withdrawn. He apologized to Bella for this. Bella remembered this and how she'd forgiven the old cat with a soothing voice and how it seemed the old guy had smiled, in that way that animals might smile.

Shortly after this there was a tension in the house both Bella and the old cat sensed. The cat had told Bella that he felt his time was nearly up and he'd be leaving her soon but he couldn't explain to Bella what this meant.

Early one morning the people put the old cat in a pet carrier and headed for the door. The old cat mewed, expressing his sadness. Bella barked a few encouraging words, telling the cat he'd be home soon. This time the cat did smile, cocked his head slightly to the side, and whispered in a barely audible voice, 'Goodbye Bella, I enjoyed our time together'. Bella remembered the knowing look in his very sad eyes. She would always remember that look.

Bella waited at the door for what seemed like forever, but when the people returned the pet carrier was empty. She often wondered what happened to her friend, but deep down she sensed that it had been 'his time'.

Bella came back from her day dream, a little too close to TW as she had picked up her pace while reminiscing. She backed off a bit and looked at TW, a sadness enveloping her as she thought about her fate, trapped in a pack with such a ruthless leader, doing whatever it took to survive. Maybe she'd try not to remember so much. Maybe that would help.

The leader of the pack, TW, was nothing more than a bully and he could be vicious with the pack. He wasn't very bright but he was the pack leader, end of story. He tolerated the dogs but often thought about replacing them. What good was Fluff he thought, as she, for some reason, nearly ran into him from behind. He'd like to replace her and that useless Slow but there weren't any other options.

A couple other dog packs had formed but they had ran them out of their territory, you couldn't find a dog without a pack these days. So he tolerated the dogs, as long as they kept in line. He'd growl and stand over them menacingly if they ever dared give him any grief. He glanced across the road at Shep, the exception. How'd he love to tear into that dog, he put up with more from Shep that all of the other dogs combined. Shep had value and he knew it.

TW glanced back after Fluff had nearly ran into him. The other dogs were in their usual places, Rat and

Fluff side by side right behind him, a little ways back came Goldie and then Slow on his heels. It appeared that Goldie had once again been encouraging Slow to keep up. TW didn't much care for the relationship between Goldie and Slow but at least they weren't falling behind. He glanced back once more to scowl at Slow then focused his attention ahead and on the trip back to the den.

None suffered TW's wrath more than Slow. He was the oldest and the recent cold had been hard on him. He once had a shiny black coat and clear brown eyes, a happy dog that loved playing with his family. Now his eyes had dimmed and his coat was dull and filthy. He was always trailing behind the pack, his hips hurt him and it made it hard to keep up.

Slow missed his people family terribly. He was a very friendly dog, one of those dogs that wanted to be a lap dog but was just too big. Good natured and gentle, he had grown up with his family's kids and was wonderful around them, even when they were small.

Now those characteristics worked against him, they weren't survival characteristics. He wasn't made for all this pack stuff, his family had been his pack. There had never been threats and violence with his people pack. They were all he knew, he'd lived with them since he was a tiny puppy, barely even remembering his mother and littermates.

TW had teased him once about being a 'nice guy' and this was no time for nice guys. TW was a killer and he bragged often about this, even though the pack rarely killed. They had been living mostly off what they could scavenge. The farmers hadn't had time to harvest their crops before all the people disappeared so the dogs found beans and corn to eat in the fields. On occasion they would stumble across the remains of a coyote kill.

The people were gone before the annual deer hunting season too. There were many deer, living off the bounty of the farmers fields. With people gone the deer had become less shy and would often be seen out gleaning the fields during the day. Coyotes, also unhindered by their fear of people, had been hunting them. The dog pack got the leftovers.

The dogs did once corner an older doe who had somehow come up lame. This was the kill TW bragged about often. Slow had once thought about pointing out that the only way they were able to kill the deer was because it was lame and nearly dead anyway, but he quickly put it out of his mind, unwilling to give TW another reason to hate him. He knew that TW wasn't very bright but he tried his best to appease the bigger, younger dog because he got the feeling that TW would like to someday brag about killing him.

They were becoming a wild pack and it hadn't taken that long. Slow hated being part of the pack but his will to survive had taken over and he went along. He also hated his nickname. In his mind he'd tried to keep his real name alive, but it had slipped away. There wasn't much time to think and reminisce, they were all falling deeper and deeper into survival mode. Finding a place in the pack, killing, scavenging, living. He speculated whether they would hold on to any of their former lives and what would happen if they were ever reunited with their families.

Slow was working hard to stay with the pack, buoyed by Goldie's encouraging words. He was so very thankful to have a friend like Goldie, friends sometimes made the most intolerable situations tolerable. Goldie was just ahead of him and he did his best to stay with him.

Goldie, like Slow and Fluff, also missed his people family very much. He was glad for his friend Slow. Having someone of like mind to chat with during down times was invaluable to Goldie. He was glad to have a friend.

His forever home also had cats, two of them. He'd always liked the cats and often enjoyed chatting with them, they offered such a different perspective. The people were nice and they were his pack but the cats were his only friends. It seemed the only problem they ever had was when he'd eat the poo out of the cats' litter box. The people would inexplicably shout at him and shoo him out into the fenced in backyard. There he'd sit and ponder what all the commotion was about.

The cats they'd chased up a tree today, they reminded him of his old friends. He'd been very nervous about the whole situation. What was going to happen? Where they actually going to kill those poor cats. They looked so helpless and afraid stuck up in that tree. He'd circled the tree and barked a few times, got to keep up appearances you know, but secretly he was hoping for a miracle.

Then that squirrel showed up and they'd given chase. When they got back and heard Slow tell about how the cats had escaped his first thought was that TW was going to kill Slow and there was nothing he could do about it. Then he looked at Slow, and the tracks under the tree, and speculated that maybe the cats 'escape' had been a little more arranged than Slow had let on. He decided then and there that he wouldn't try to pry the lid off of that can of worms, he would just let Slow keep his little secret. If TW ever suspected anything, that would be the end of Slow for sure.

Other then the run in today with the cats Goldie wasn't too troubled being part of the pack. He enjoyed being out and about, exploring and looking for food. He'd been a pretty sad dog before joining the pack, he had missed his family terribly.

The hardest part of everything was TW. If you got on the wrong side of that dog you'd be in big trouble. He spent lots of time trying to appease TW and help keep Slow out of trouble. He knew TW had it in for Slow so it made for a tricky situation, trying to help Slow, being his friend, yet not irking TW.

For the most part it appeared that TW tolerated and maybe even approved of their buddy system. Maybe he even knew that Goldie was helping Slow keep up and fit in with the pack. To Goldie it would be surprising if TW figured anything out because, and Goldie would never say this out loud, but, well, TW just wasn't very bright.

Goldie looked up to see they were fairly close to Fluff and Rat, Slow was doing a good job of keeping up today. He didn't much care for the smaller dogs, they were both huge sycophants. Fluff was annoying but wasn't much trouble and really never worried him but that other dog, the black, curly haired terrier mutt Rat, now that dog made him nervous. If any in the pack could challenge TW for pure viciousness it was Rat.

Rat heard the other dogs and glanced back, surprised to see Slow and Goldie so close behind. He chuckled to himself, figuring that TW had put the fear of God into Slow after he'd lost the cats. Slow better toe the line or TW would tear him to pieces. He'd gladly be a part of that show.

Rat ran proudly, chest out, barely panting, staying right on TW's heals. He thought of himself as TW's right hand man. That dog Shep had no right to be the packs number two, he was always causing trouble for TW. Rat would like to tear into him too. In fact, besides TW, there were times he'd like to tear into all the other dogs, with the possible exception of Fluff. Fluff seemed to share his interest in backing TW in all things.

Rat rarely thought of his people family anymore. It's not that he didn't like them, after all they were once his pack. He remembered living with them and always being on guard, protecting his pack. On occasion other people besides his family would approach their house, some he knew, some were complete strangers. It didn't matter, he'd always react the same way.

This was his packs' house, when he heard someone bang on the front door he'd shoot like a bullet and slam into the door, barking as viciously as he could. In the summer, when only the screen door stood between him and the intruder, he'd hit the screen on the lower part of the door at a dead run, hoping to break through. The door was damaged and the screen bowed out from his constant assaults. He often got scolded by his people but he didn't care, this was his pack and his home and he wouldn't tolerate any others.

Now this was his pack, nothing else mattered. Rat prided himself on being a valued member of his new pack. His value had never been on more display then when he helped run off other packs. He remembered running full tilt at one bigger dog, a leader of another pack, slamming into him at full speed and sending him sprawling across the ground. The entire pack had run off after this, never to be heard from again.

Rat was entirely fearless and completely devoted to his pack and the pack leader TW. He would follow TW anywhere and do anything TW asked without question. In his mind TW was the greatest leader the world had ever known. He was tough and vicious and strong and mean. And he was very bright! To Rat it seemed TW was nearly perfect. Rat puffed out his chest a little more and picked up his pace. He was now so close to TW he could smell what the bigger dog had had for breakfast.

It was getting dark out by the time they reached the Den. They had stopped several times along the way, gleaning what they could from the bean field, tearing away at what little meat was left on a rotting deer carcase, presumably killed by the coyotes, and getting a nice long drink at a small stream. The water was cold and clean. The air and water had both improved dramatically since the people had left.

As far as the food went, they hadn't found enough, all of them were still hungry by the time they reached the Den. The excursions of chasing cats and a squirrel, with no satisfaction, had taken a lot out of the pack.

The Den was a house near the back of a typical subdivision, lots of houses, all abandoned now. The roads curved this way and that but the dogs all knew the way.

When they arrived home the dogs went directly inside and headed for soft, warm beds. They made their beds in the main floor living room, hardly ever using any other part of the house. If they had to go potty they did that outside in the front yard, which was becoming a very large mess. At least they didn't go inside, this part of being pets they hadn't forgotten.

There were many groans and sighs as the dogs made themselves comfortable. Once they had settled in

TW talked about going back after the cats early the next morning. He wanted to take his time, go slow until they spotted the cats. His goal was to see them before being seen. Then they would split into two groups with one group chasing the cats right into the waiting jaws of the other group. Shep raised his eyebrows, surprised that TW's plan was actually sound. The other dogs just wanted to rest, they were only half heartedly paying attention.

Shep decided to make an objection, as he so often did. In animal speak he said they should forget about the cats for now and go on a hunt, they could use TW's plan with larger game that could make a good meal for the pack. In the background Rat growled his disapproval.

TW stood and also growled. He wanted only the cats and was not in the mood to hear opinions from others.

Shep, maybe a little unwisely, pressed on. Going after the cats would make a meal for maybe two of the pack, but not all. The pack needed to head toward the fields and find another deer, either lame or a recent coyote kill. At least there'd be beans and corn if they couldn't find a deer.

To this TW replied with body language, stepping towards Shep, growling menacingly. Shep realized it was an ego thing now, TW's ego had been doubly bruised, not only by the cats but by the squirrel. Shep didn't care, he pressed on.

He didn't agree with this, the cats would take too much time and be too much work. He moved a bit further away from TW and let the other dog know that he was fine with being kicked out of the pack but he couldn't agree with spending another day, the entire pack hungry and tired, chasing two elusive cats.

The standoff continued for a few minutes. Shep had known what he was going to say and had guessed at TW's reaction so he had positioned himself near the door. If TW attacked he was leaving and if somehow he was cornered and had to fight he was ready.

It was a fight he knew he couldn't win outright but if he could maim one of TW's legs, then run off, maybe he could lead TW away, and circle back to the pack. Then he would see if any wanted to go with him, he figured all but Rat would. Then off they would go, leaving TW and Rat behind. It would be doubtful if TW could survive lame. It was a different world now. With the humans the dogs could survive terrible injuries with a trip to the vet. Now, the smallest injury could be the end of them.

He knew TW was stronger but he was quicker, it would be a simple matter to dodge TW's initial attack, tear at a hind leg as he passed, and sprint out of the bigger dogs reach. With luck he could inflict a serious enough injury that TW would be helpless. It wouldn't matter how big and tough he was if he was limping along on three legs. That kind of injury would be the death of him.

If he wasn't able to injure him that seriously then he hoped that at least he would slow him down enough that he could make a break for it. If his plan didn't work out he figured he'd be able to survive well enough on his own. He was really tired of TW and was ready to take a big risk to be rid of him. He crouched, ready for the attack.

The standoff continued. TW had stopped growling but he continued to stand his ground, trying to stare Shep down. The other dogs watched with bated breath, it was a very tense situation. Unfortunately for TW the shepherd wasn't easily intimidated.

Eventually TW walked to his spot on the floor and curled up. This was how many confrontations between him and Shep ended. TW saying nothing, no one agreeing with anyone, one or the other eventually just walking away.

The dogs settled in, best they could. For many of them this would be a restless night, hungry and cold. Rat and Fluff huddled together for warmth, Glodie and Slow slept back to back, also sharing some body heat.

All of the dogs woke now and then during the long night. Some went outside to relieve themselves. Others went to the basement and drank from the pool that had formed down there. The cold water was refreshing and helped to relieve their hunger pains somewhat. After taking care of whatever business they thought needed tending to they would once again settle down in their makeshift beds and try to sleep. There were many groans and sighs throughout the night.

The next day they were all up very early. Without a word they headed for the fields in search of deer, or maybe just beans.

Chapter 10

At about the time TW and Shep were having their little standoff the cats were just waking from a little cat nap. They had heard nothing of the dogs for some time and had settled in quite comfortably in their hiding place. Now they were both peering out the dirty window at the setting sun, a cold white dot on the horizon. It was going to be a chilly night.

Feeling fairly sure the dogs were gone for the night they decided to make their way back to the farm and meet up with Prince. They would have liked to go home and sleep but they were very hungry. They were cautious during the short trip, picking their way slowly from one hiding spot to the next, looking around corners before moving, smelling the cold December air, listening for sounds of the night. There were so few.

They heard the hoot of an owl which caused them both to crouch down low under the branches of a small pine tree. Sasha once had a close call with a large great horned owl. She had told Ava the story several times as they lounged in the sun back when they were comfortably living in their forever home.

It had been a warm summer night, lit by a waxing gibbous moon. Sasha was an outdoor kitty at the time and she was tracking a field mouse at the edge of a nearby woods. The moon was low in the sky behind her and she cast an eerily elongated shadow ahead.

She had been fascinated at the movements of her shadow as she crept along when suddenly her shadow transformed into a great winged beast. Frightened by this abrupt change she had, with one mighty spring from her powerful hind legs, shot behind a large tree. Her head swivelled quickly back to the spot she had vacated, just in time to see an enormous bird swoop past.

She remembered marveling at how quiet the bird had been, she only heard a slight rushing of the air when the owl was mere feet from her. The quiet was disturbed when the owl called back to her, hooting out something that sounded suspiciously like 'I'll get you next time little kitty'.

Ava had heard this story many times and, the more she heard it, the more she had scoffed. Why would a bird chase a cat she would ask, this didn't make any sense at all. Ava's experience with birds amounted to watching them bounce about the bird feeders as she enjoyed a lazy afternoon on the back of a chair. This owl couldn't be any bigger than the wild turkeys that sometimes visited the front yard, pecking at the ground under the feeders.

These birds were huge but they were jittery and nervous. Ava had often frightened them by springing into the window, banging against the glass and bouncing back down into her chair. Oh how she had chuckled at their reaction as they clucked and ran away, stopping after a few yards to gaze back at the window with looks of disdain given to their tormenter.

After hearing Sasha pour through this old story she would often tell of the time she had been in the backyard, before Sasha came to live with them, and had snagged a bird, in full flight, right out of the air. Sasha would listen to this story and smile, it was Ava's only catch, other than the mountain of cat toys she would 'catch' while playing with their people. She didn't begrudge Ava her moment of glory and would politely listen to her story while remembering the days, sometimes a week at a time, when her first people would be gone or forget to put out food and she would be forced to catch mice and sometimes birds for her supper. These were too numerous to count.

The cats waited several minutes before moving, and were even more cautious. Ava wasn't scoffing about any of Sasha's old stories anymore. The hoot hoot of the owl had made them both doubly nervous.

It was quite dark out by the time they made it to the farmhouse, Prince calling out to them from the front porch, once again before he'd been seen. Up on the porch the girls begin to tell about their trouble with the dogs. Prince said he had observed most of what happened but admitted he'd been at a loss as to how to help the cats. Out of desperation he'd planning on calling out to the dogs and hoping they'd all chase him, and he'd hide under one of the barns. He'd figured that this would probably fail as the dogs would leave a guard, he didn't know about Slow of course.

However, the squirrel took over this task and Prince could only watch as events unfolded. The girls had also told Prince about the owl. He said he'd heard him and they were right to be cautious, he was a dangerous creature. After this the cats all agreed they should stay together even more, hopefully there was safety in numbers. The bonds of their small pack grew.

That night they spent hunting the barns. The cold was driving the rodents out of the fields and into the shelter of any buildings they could find. More snow had fallen and they could see the little paths the rodents had made as they scurried for shelter. This was great for the cats, not only to get out of the weather but also to be less exposed, while hunting rodents, to anything that might be hunting them!

They were done hunting long before dawn. It was a cold, crisp, windless and moonlit night. As always, very quiet. Prince invited Sasha and Ava to accompany him inside the farmhouse. They crept across the barnyard, up the porch steps, and through the rip in the screen door.

Inside they found the home to be comforting. It was dusty and the furniture was old, but it had a nice old farmhouse smell and the cats felt safe. Prince gave them a quick tour and told them they were more then welcome to sleep over, if they'd like. Sasha and Ava glanced at each other. Except for a night at the vet neither had spent any time away from home since they'd been adopted by their forever family. But they were tired and, well, times were different now. It was practical and safe to stay here, for a little while.

Prince led them to a bedroom with an unusually tall bed. He told them he liked this room because it had two doors, which meant two routes of escape. The cats leapt up on the bed and snuggled in for a good mornings sleep.

From this time on the cats would spend most of their time together, staying at the farm but on occasion napping at Sasha and Ava's home. For the girls it was hard to let go of home. Plus the food bag was still there and, although they never ate more than what amounted to a small snack, it was still comforting to know it existed, just in case they really needed it.

Time passed and soon it had been an uneventful week or more since Sasha and Ava had been home. The weather had turned colder and the snow a little deeper. In

98

Sasha's humble opinion even a fine dusting of snow was too deep, much more so the several inches now on the ground. With the cold weather the cats had taken to hunting exclusively inside. There were several buildings on the farm and they had no shortage of prey.

However, home is where the heart is and eventually the cats wanted to go back for a visit. Prince had been reluctant at first, he reasoned that they had everything they needed right where they were, and they were safe. The cats countered and made many good points, Sasha and Ava's home wasn't far, many nearby homes had become rodent infested, and the cat food, couldn't forget about that. Back and forth they went, but in the end they all agreed to make the short trip.

There were many good points, for and against, and the cats considered them all. One point they didn't consider is that cats just like an adventure, this is what really made up their minds, whether they'd admit it or not.

It was the middle of the night when they set out, the best time for cats to go prowling. It was slow going, they were all very cautious and alert, listening and watching for any sign of the dog pack or any other dangers. They hadn't seen or heard the pack in a while, the dogs were long overdue to make an appearance, although it was very doubtful they would be out and about at this time of night.

Off in the distance they heard a few coyotes howling, they were a long ways away and shouldn't be a problem. Lately, they had heard the coyotes howling more and more, maybe this was why the dogs were staying away. The cats had found no sign of coyotes near the farmhouse or surrounding barns but they used this threat as a reason to stay inside even more.

It was still dark and no birds were near, no air support at night. They missed having the birds to help them watch for trouble. Since they'd been more nocturnal they hadn't interacted much with the birds.

They crept across the road, so strange to see it covered in undisturbed snow. Looking back and forth, as if they were checking for traffic, they all noticed the ironic beauty. The pavement truly looked as if it were covered with a fine white blanket, perfectly laid out and tucked in at the edges, smooth and even as if someone had spent a good deal of time making this particular bed. Quite possibly the only time the road had ever looked more peaceful than the surrounding landscape. The peaceful beauty of it all countered by the danger of the new world they found themselves in.

Quickly they scampered across, their tracks a glaring imperfection on the once nearly perfect snow covering.

There was a strong smell in the air, the cats had noticed it from the farmhouse, and it got stronger as they approached home. It was skunk smell, even Ava knew that. Judging by the smell, they were sure the skunk had been in their house. Most animals of this size should be hibernating by now, winter was here.

They cautiously entered, no one was there. If the skunk had been inside, he didn't seem to have stayed. Or maybe he was curled up in some dark corner. None of the cats wanted to find him. Soon they noticed the food bag, it was dragged out into the middle of the first room they entered and it was torn and tattered. They found a few nuggets of cat food but that was basically the end of the back up supply. Maybe it was the skunk but likely a combination of wild animals. Their old home had been discovered and it was wild lands now, hardly a home at all.

They sat and stared at the bag in silence. A kind of cat sadness stole over them. The safety net was gone. More importantly, maybe not survival important, but that kind of importance that we hand out to something that signifies a changing of the times, Sasha and Ava both realized this meant the end of their dependence on the humans. They were truly on their own now. Something clicked inside, they were becoming more and more like wild animals. The cats left the house, they were moving on.

They spent some time hunting a couple of open neighbor homes and had great success. The rodent population had exploded, feasting on the food stocks the humans had left behind. Soon they were full and tired and it was well past time to go back to the farm, a morning cat-nap long overdue.

Dawn had come, followed by a cold and gray morning, like many winter days in Michigan. Even after the sun had been up for several hours it would still seem distant and too far south and provide about as much warmth as a candle on the wrong side of a window.

This time of year it was hard to find many differences between night and day. The days were cold, the nights were colder. The days were dreary, the sun rarely poking through the thick gray cloud cover. The darkness of the night hardly a difference to the cats with their superior night vision. But night was safer, the cats understood this, they were becoming more nocturnal, more the way nature made them. With the dawn it was time to go, day made the cats uneasy, so off they went.

As they made their way back toward the farmhouse Sasha and Ava both took a moment to look back at the old home. Again that cat sadness was in their eyes. Yes, they were moving on, but that was once home, and a gentle homesickness swept over them both. Soon they turned and continued on towards the farm. Where they were going, that was what had to be done.

Chapter 11

January passed fairly uneventfully for the little cat pack and the bigger dog pack. It had been a snowy month and that made travel very difficult so they didn't see much of each other.

TW was forced to ignore his beef with the cats and concentrate on survival. The dogs spent a lot of time in fields around the den digging in the snow for beans. Recently they'd had another successful deer hunt, of these there hadn't been many.

If it had been up to TW to tell the story then it would have sounded like they were the bravest, best hunting dog pack that ever existed. The truth of it was that a large doe with a broken front leg had been found by the pack. She must have gotten tangled in some fallen branches covered by snow and snapped the leg, it dangled awkwardly as she hopped about.

The dogs had spotted her at a distance, easy game they had all thought, except, of course, Shep. He'd seen what wild animals could do when the end was near.

The dogs came at a run, no strategy involved. The doe was at the edge of a wood and entered as soon as she saw them coming. When they were closing in for the kill the doe took off at a dead run, leaving them in the dust, or snow, as it were. They were amazed and slowed, entering the woods at a trot. How had this animal, with a severely broken front leg, taken off at a run? A wild animal can do things outside of the understanding of people or house pets when life is threatened.

They picked up her trail, easy in the snowy woods, and followed. Soon they saw a flash of her in the distance and the chase was on. They quickly caught up with her and found her lying in a slight depression of the earth, her bad leg pointing in an impossible direction. Adrenaline can take you only so far, and the doe was spent. TW approached and the doe attempted to jump up. It stumbling on her bad leg and he launched at her throat. To his credit he made it quick. Dinner was served.

It wasn't quite that easy for the dogs. They had to work at it very hard, the doe had a thick winter coat. One of the smaller dogs attempted to disembowel the animal a little too far back and released a unbelievable stench. Dogs this didn't bother, people would have been a different story.

They worked at the deer for a long time, biting, tearing and also growling and barking at each other. Eventually they had all eaten their fill with a fair amount left, they'd come back tomorrow and scavenge, if there was anything left to scavenge.

They'd become quite adept at scavenging, having come across several half-eaten kills they could only assume were made by coyotes. The deer were well fed and abundant, the result of people leaving before hunting season and before harvest. The kills, if you'd have been looking, were almost always lame deer. Injuries happen in the wild, many are fatal, wild animals don't have vets.

It was a difficult and intense life for the dog pack. Sometimes they went hungry. Sometimes they had to work very hard for a meal. It was an interesting life but it would be a stretch to call it fun. This could be attributed partly to TW. TW would never be thought of as fun.

Fun wasn't something that happened anymore. This was only a fond memory of a time long ago when they still lived with their people. TW never came right out and said there will be no more fun, he just didn't tolerate any fooling around. No fun, the other dogs understood. But why not, when you're digging for damn beans in a field, have some fun with it. It's not like you're going to scare away the beans or find fewer. Sometimes fewer, when you've eaten nothing but beans for days, seems a little better.

Ahh leadership, often more important to impose one's will then worry about such trivial things like enjoying life at no cost. That was the dilemma the dogs all found themselves in, hide your smiles, hide your happiness, your leader might find these things inappropriate. Your leader, forced upon you by circumstance.

It wasn't all about TW though. The dogs found ways to make life more tolerable despite him. That's what one had to do when circumstance put you with intolerable leadership. So often leadership did not understand the roll circumstance played and deserving thoughts took over. This would often lead to trouble. But the dogs did what they could to tolerate TW and make the best of their situation.

There were the rabbit hunts. Rat and Shep had figured this out. Rat was adept at wiggling into tight places, fighting his way into the undergrowth with ease. Fluff was his understudy and did her best to help out. Shep would position himself at the other side of whatever pile Rat was working his way into, and be there to snap the necks of unsuspecting scared, cute little bunny rabbits. Nature's a bitch.

Goldie and Slow had taken to each other. For entertainment they conversed about everything. Sometimes, having someone that can actually have a conversation is about the most valuable thing you can have. Easy to find someone that wants to tell their stories but someone that can go back and forth, much more difficult.

As for TW, lording over others and being worshiped was his entertainment. Although it would be hard to call fear and intimidation worship, they somewhat resembled each other. Rat was probably the closest that came to worship. He didn't much care for Rat and Shep forming the bunny alliance, this took a little away from Rat worshiping him, but he never said anything. He liked the taste of cute little bunnies.

TW didn't listen to a word Goldie and Slow had to say, conversation was useless in his mighty opinion. Why would anyone talk about how breathtaking the stars would appear on a moonless, cloudless night, or the intricate beauty of millions of snowflakes drifting to earth, or the simple enthralling movement of a plastic bag caught in an updraft...well, maybe not that last one, but you get the idea. This was all beyond TW. Sometimes he would see them talking and walk by, bumping Slow into a drift, and he'd laugh. Being a bully, that was his thing.

TW had been satisfied with the packs routine but the cats still lingered in the back of his mind. Travel, hunting, finding food in the fields, it had all been very difficult as the snow continued to pile up and the deep cold of winter had the land firmly in its icy grip.

He had led the pack on a few expeditions in the general direction of the cats, but he no longer talked about his ultimate goal. They would get side tracked with a hunt or digging in a field then end up heading back to the Den as night approached. His plan was to, one day, get them so far out that they wouldn't be able to make it back to the Den by night fall. Then he would lead them on towards the cats with the ruse of finding shelter for the night. One of these days.

As for the cats, they were surviving okay. Hunting at the farm had become more difficult, the rodent population was dwindling. There were some rats and this helped make up for the decline in mice. They occasionally crossed the road to Sasha and Ava's old neighborhood when they could. It was a challenging journey, made more strenuous by the winter snows. When they made it they found the hunting to be much better then at the farm. If the people could see their houses now, overrun with rodents and stinking of mouse piss, how positively sad they would be.

The cats kept up their guard but didn't have many problems being hunted themselves. In recent weeks coyotes had shown up a couple of times at the farm but never lingered. They heard the dogs once or twice but hadn't seen them in a while. They had a den far away and winter wasn't conducive to travel. There were no other dog packs around, this didn't bode well for all the dogs that had been left behind by their people. The cats didn't mind.

Cold, it was always cold. They slept together, underneath a great comforter on an old bed. They went out only at night. Dark, cold, slow, that was how the winter was passing.

This routine rarely changed. Occasionally they would come across a hibernating animal or the winter drifts would alter their paths to a house they'd never been to before, but mostly it was the same old thing. Hunt, seek shelter, keep warm, survive. There were no friendly human hands to pet them, no warm laps to nap in, no soothing voices in the night, these things were all distant memories. It was a cold, hard world, the cats did their best.

Chapter 12

Winter seemed like it would never end. The cold, short dreary days. Snow and more snow. Lately the winds had been whipping it up into great drifts, blocking some of their paths to the different barns. It made hunting that much harder, as if it weren't hard enough going out in the snow and cold each and every night.

The rodent population at the farm was definitely on a downturn, from overhunting mostly. The cats had occasionally made their way across the road to hunt Sasha and Ava's old neighborhood, and each time the girls would make a case for staying. Prince was hesitant, to him the farmhouse was the safest place for them with its many hiding places. He did say that he was open to moving if they could find a house as safe as the farmhouse. Rodent hunting the many houses was much easier but so far they hadn't found a house that seemed like it would be as safe as the farm.

It wasn't very far from the farmhouse to Sasha and Ava's house, but the trip was hard. They would scamper a short way on top of crusted old snow only to find their path blocked by a huge drift. They would then either double back or try to find a way around it. It seemed like each time they made the trip the path would change, like a maze puzzle with ever shifting sides.

This night the path led them a little ways away from the girls' old home, they found a house they hadn't been in before. Another broken out window, easy access. The house was teeming with mice, mice that had mostly never been hunted. It was easy pickings and the cats were soon full to bursting.

Ava had asked if they shouldn't just sleep here. Prince wouldn't hear of it. It was the excess food making them lazy. They needed to go home. Ava thought that he was really attached to the old farmhouse. Maybe he was.

On the short journey back to the farm a distant howl was heard, a few even more distant barks answered, what could be going on with the canine menace? Soon they were home and snuggled into the warm bed. It was very cold in the house but the cats fur had thickened enormously, keeping them quite comfortable. Forgetting the distant barks and howls they slept long and soundly.

Sasha awoke with a start. A bark in the farmyard, the dog pack was here, she quickly woke the other two. The cats found perches to peer out the windows, Ava the last to stir and find a spot.

Crouching low, they caught glimpses of the dog pack running about the farmyard sniffing and searching. Most likely it was cat scent they were following, an ominous but obvious conclusion. Prince whispered to Sasha and Ava, be calm, we're fine. It was a simple cat sound with which he conveyed the message, one which the other cats understood instinctively, without thought. That is why the humans never quite understood the animals, humans couldn't understand simple and they were far far removed from their instincts.

It wasn't only calm that Prince had conveyed, but also confidence. They had all explored every inch of the house and knew a hundred escape routes. If the dogs gained entry into the house the cats were confident they could escape.

As they watched the dogs scamper to and fro, appearing to aimlessly rush about the yard following scents back and forth in a frenzy of activity, it occurred to Prince that the dogs were an unorganized lot of amature hunters and he questioned how they had survived this long. TW, the leader, was in the wildest frenzy of them all.

In this way the dogs were like their human masters, emulating their silly leaders. If the leader was a narcissist that was always in a frenzy then so would be the fools that followed. The frenzy part anyway. The dogs seemed at least smart enough to know to feed the ego and make everything about their leader. Thus, as TW would rush towards a corner of one of the outbuildings growling and snapping, one of his minions would observe and quickly copy the routine, securing his or her place in the pecking order.

This continued for some time giving the cats a rare moment of amusement. Sheep? or dogs? They wondered. And how was it the dogs never seemed to look up. Did they not know 'up'? Not once had they looked to see if anyone was observing them from above. For that matter none of them had even ventured onto the houses' front porch, much less thought to gain entry to the house. This was very curious to the cats, their scent had to be strongest at the porch. What was keeping them away?

Prince mentioned that the dogs appeared to have no thoughts past their leader and would only dare do anything on his command. It was like there was only one dog. The others would either do their best to imitate TW's berserker frenzy, or if not capable of this would cower away from the action and try to do exactly what they thought might be expected of them. If they could not figure out what might be expected of them, then doing nothing at all seemed to be best. This is what the golden retriever, the little fluffy white dog and the older lab eventually did, standing together in the middle of the yard, while TW rushed about, the little black terrier so close he'd frequently bump into TW's behind.

The shepherd mix was the one that really concerned the cats. Sure he was also growling, barking, snarling, but it appeared to only be for show and with a edge of amusement. Like he was mocking TW. The shepherd was methodical in his approach and had circled the yard never going back to the same place twice, unlike TW and the black terrier, whom had now threatened every building, tree, bush, and even an old burning barrel many times.

TW had barked at the shepherd repeatedly, obviously attempting to get the dog in line and follow him and the terrier around and around on their berserker merry go round. The shepherd would turn and follow, but only a step or two, then back to his search.

At one point the shepherd had been sniffing around the front porch but TW called him off. For some unknown reason, TW would not approach the house. He'd always seen the cats outside and quite possibly he simply couldn't comprehend that they might be inside. After all he wasn't very bright. It had been no easy matter for TW to get the shepherd in line, he'd gotten right in the other dogs face, ready for an all out dog fight.

The shepherd had stood his ground for a moment, appearing to weigh his options, a look in his eyes of hate and disdain for the other dog. He appeared to be coldly calculating his chances, positioning himself for a lunge. A look that said he could take him, hurt him, maybe hurt him real bad.

It wasn't long and the standoff was over, the shepherd must have concluded that he'd probably also get hurt, maybe badly. He followed TW towards the middle of the yard, towards three of the other dogs which immediately began to cower in anticipation of their leader's rath.

As they walked away the shepherd looked back and up, meeting the cats eyes.

This sent the cats into a tense crouch, chills running up and down their bodies. They were discovered. The shepherd knew. Why he wasn't attempting to inform the other dogs of this they had no idea. He could have simply told TW the cats were in the house, there was no need for a confrontation. Why he chose not to was a mystery to the cats, probably something to do with their seemingly contentious relationship.

Once again Prince comforted the other cats. Yes, the shepherd mix might know, but it was highly unlikely he would be able to overcome his leader's stupidity and, oddly, he didn't seem to even want to try. The cats worked up the nerve to, very carefully, peer out the window again.

They watched as TW and the black terrier joined the other dogs in the middle of the yard. The shepherd had wandered off, in total disregard of his leaders commands, and was gazing out into one of the fields. The other five dogs were huddled close together and appeared to be discussing their next move.

Darkness was creeping over the farm, chasing away the gray day. It was hard to tell the difference between night and day at a time like this. The cats were still tired from not enough sleep. Although they had slept the day away, this far north and at this time of year there just wasn't much day to sleep away. Sasha thought that this might be why the winter seemed to be so hard on people. They were daytime creatures and needed the light.

As the dogs gathered in the barnyard, Sasha recalled many nights watching her bumbling people stumble around in the dark. She sometimes would silently follow them as they bumped and thudded about, finally switching on a blinding light that cause Sasha to scurry for a hiding spot.

She had noticed the horribly abrupt light would totally change the demeanor of her people. Just as quickly as the flicking of a light switch would chase away the comfortable darkness, so to would it transform her people. The outstretched arms would lower to more normal positions, the knees would begin to bend again, and they would move about much more normally. Normal movement for them was still clumsy and slow but Sasha very much disliked the night time version of her people as they reminded her of the gore covered monsters that appeared in some of the scary movies her little girl loved to watch.

Sasha concluded that people were night blind. Prince agreed with this assessment. Ava didn't care one bit, she thought people were sometimes so stupid as nearly impossible to bear. She remembered the looks she would give them, utter disdain. Always she would be surprised at their reactions, cooing and fawning over her, obviously totally unable to pick up on what she was laying down. Clueless, that's what Ava thought, much like the dogs that had been circling the farm yard, barking at nothing, without purpose or direction.

Ava missed her people but sometimes their constant chatter was much worse than Mr Squirrel, and the inability to ever be satisfied with the current situation was annoying. She often told them, with a quick look, that it was time to relax.

It was hard for Ava to grasp that they couldn't pick up on her simple signals. Yes, she missed them, but she remembered many times thinking that she wished they were trainable. She wanted to teach them how to sit in the dark and enjoy listening to the quiet night. The only times they would do that were when that noisy glowing box was lit up, then they would sit and stare at it for hours, mesmerized. She hated that thing and often would lurk about behind it trying to figure out where the images came from and maybe find a way to scare them off.

Ava remembered more then once sitting and watching her people as that magic box took them over, puzzled at how they would drift into a semi-catatonic state. Frustrated that right out the nearest window was a great wide world to explore and they would just sit, transfixed. Ava concluded that this may have been how they slept.

The cats musings and reflections were interrupted by a nearby howl. The dogs were now all in the main yard between the house and biggest of the barns, grouped together, watching. Soon two coyotes appeared at the edge of the yard, coming out of the field from the south. A standoff ensued with much growling and howling and barking.

The coyotes slowly advanced and appeared ready to attack. TW wanted to stand his ground, he didn't care, he was ready for a fight. Surprisingly Shep joined him and let out a menacing sound that was somewhere between a hiss and a growl. The other dogs were too frightened to approach the coyotes.

Soon the small pack of former pets backed away and conceded the area to the coyotes. The dog pack was becoming more and more like a pack of wild animals but these two were true wild animals and they were fearless with hunger. Their wild eyes and deliberate approach were more than enough to convince the dogs to flee. The coyotes did not pursue the dogs, losing interest as soon as they'd left, and began exploring the barnyard.

Watching this all unfold from their hiding spot high up in the old farmhouse the cats had hardly dared even breath. The coyotes appeared to catch a rat near the barn, ripping and tearing. They continued hunting for some time then slinked off from whence they came, never coming near the house. The cats breathed a deep sigh of relief as the coyotes disappeared back into the darkness. They felt very fortunate that these wild animals hadn't come for them, they probably still had some fear of human dwellings. It had taken a long time before they had come this close.

They would spend some time lounging in the bedroom, alternately looking out the window and chatting amongst themselves. Although still tired sleep would not come. There had been too much excitement to allow for that. Night had come and, taking a cue from their rumbling bellies, they decided it was time to hunt

Chapter 14

The dogs had run for some time after leaving the farm. After using up the adrenaline from the confrontation with the coyotes they had slowed to a trot and eventually came to a halt amongst the poor shelter of a line of tall pine trees. They were somewhere about half way between the cats and home.

Night was coming and they were all anxious to get back to the Den and cuddle up for warmth, but they needed a break to gather themselves and get their wind back.

TW was in a fine state, silent and sullen. Even Rat sensed it would be unwise to approach his leader at this time. None dared ask TW when they would be starting back up for home, they just assumed he would lead on after they'd rested a bit.

To the other dogs surprise TW curled up under one of the pine trees. He didn't appear to be attempting to sleep, his eyes were darting about, he was agitated. The other dogs paired off and got as comfortable as possible. Rat and Fluff snuggling in a little depression on a pine needle bed, the other three lay tightly together at the base of another pine tree next to the one TW was under, giving their leader a little space.

TW thought about the barnyard, he was sure the cats were there, he could smell them everywhere. That damn Shep knew something and he wasn't telling. He had just about had enough of that dog. He'd been so very close to attacking him when he was sniffing around the old farmhouse. Did he think he was going to go in and get a nice treat from the people? Well, Shep, the people are gone, he thought to himself.

He knew Shep was smarter than him but he didn't care much about that. It made him mad that he wouldn't do what he wanted, always had an argument, always had a reason. He wished all the dogs could be like Rat. Rat seemed to always know what he wanted without even being told.

TW knew it was likely the little pack would not have survived this long without the shepherd mixes cunning and, because of this, he tolerated him. He hated not being blindly followed, not being feared, but, deep down inside, a thought he couldn't put into words, he hated being dependent on Shep most of all.

Things had changed. The pack, all of them, with the possible exception of that useless Slow, had learned how to survive. TW figured they could now survive without Shep. He hoped. Shep could be useful if he'd just get in line, but it didn't appear that was ever going to happen.

Ever since they'd left the farm he had been mulling over chasing the shepherd off. One thing was holding him back. He might have imagined it but he could have sworn the coyotes paused when Shep had joined him, baring his fangs and snarling at the coyotes. Something wild and vicious had come out in that moment. If they ran into the coyotes again they'd need that. Rat might draw blood, bite a leg or two, but Slow and Fluff and possibly Goldie, well, the coyotes looked at them like they were looking at dinner.

None of that mattered now, all he wanted was those cats. They'd made a fool of him for the last time. He didn't know how but he could sense them watching, laughing, as he raced around the farm yard searching. He swore to himself that this very night he'd feel the crunch of their bones in his mighty jaws as he tore into them.

TW settled in under the boughs of the pines, he felt no cold, only the pain of vengeance unfulfilled. The other dogs were leaving him alone, he began to formulate a plan.

The cats waited until deep into the night before they dared venture from the farmhouse. They crept out through the tear in the front screen door into the cold windless night and there they waited, listening to the night, listening to nothing, which is what they wanted to hear.

It was quiet and dark, cloudy, like always, but nary a breeze was blowing. They sat on the porch using all their senses, on full alert for any signs of danger. A night like this was not a night they wanted to venture out but they were driven by hunger.

Even Ava, who only a few short months ago couldn't wait to get outside, felt herself being pulled back towards the house by thoughts of a warm fluffy bed. Dreamily she imagined herself dining at an overflowing food bowl back at her forever home, then lazily sauntering off towards the nearest cushy chair for a long nap.

Her thoughts were brought back to the present as she listened to Prince whispering instructions. Instructions they'd heard many times before but delivered with more urgency this night. They were to listen for any hint of the coyotes or dogs. Stay close to the buildings, close to escape routes. Any sign of danger and they were to go to the nearest hiding spot, crawl way back under or climb up high, depending on the spot. Out of the reach of bigger animals that couldn't climb and couldn't get into the tight spots.

After some time they made their way across the yard and, sneaking past one barn and another smaller building, they entered a building they'd only hunted a few times before. It was small but had a loft they could get to in a hurry if threatened. They were all hoping it would be teeming with rodents and they would be in for a quick meal.

They weren't disappointed. Ava immediately nabed a mouse that was scurrying under a thin layer of straw. Prince and Sasha had kills soon after. The cold must have driven more mice inside, the hunting was good. They were reasonably successful. The place might not have been 'teeming with rodents' like many of the houses they'd hunted, but it would do.

After a while they climbed up to the loft to take a break. They sat near an old broken window and, while gazing out at the chilly landscape below, discussed recent events and, of course, what a great place this little building was to hunt.

It had been a long, cold, winter, and they all wondered when it would end. Prince said he'd noticed the sun was higher in the sky during the day, from his experience this meant that spring was coming. It sure didn't feel like it, winter had a firm grip.

They talked about all the strange and wonderful friends they'd made since their people had gone away such a long, long time ago. The birds had been probably the closest, certainly the most useful, friends they'd made. They owed this unique relationship to an early summer night, a long time ago, when Sasha showed mercy to a helpless baby bird.

The big, slow moving fish from the neighbors pond, had been a nice diversion, although they hadn't spoken since the pond had frozen over some time ago. Friendship with a fish, that had been undoubtedly the oddest friendship that had been formed. The possum in the neighbor's house was a very interesting acquaintance. They'd woken him only once more, partly by accident, as they were hunting the house a few weeks ago. He'd been congenial, not the least bit upset at being woken, and had provided them with a nice bit of interesting conversation. Miss Bunny had also seemed happy to see them on the occasions they stopped by the brush pile to visit with her. Each time they saw her she was groggy from sleep but would invite them in to sit a while and chat. She had little to say but was eager to hear news of the world outside her little house of sticks. It had been a while since they saw her as her house was now mostly buried in the snow.

Their friendship with Slow had been the saddest. He seemed like such a good dog. Now that he was with the pack led by that awful TW, they wouldn't be able to speak with him, unless they were once again stuck in a tree. If that were to happen it was highly unlikely that TW would leave Slow to guard them.

Slow had been the only dog they had befriended. Sure, they'd made the acquaintance of several back in the early days, shortly after the people had left. But, once the packs had been formed, none of these early acquaintances would speak with them. They understood, can't be seen talking with a cat, that might affect their standing in the pack.

After they had talked for some time the cats all became quite sleepy. Dawn was still a long ways off and normally they would hunt till much deeper in the night, but since they all had quite full bellies they decided to call it an early night and head back to the farmhouse to get some much needed sleep.

After carefully negotiating the climb down from the loft, a feat much more difficult then the climb up, they snuck through a broken board and stepped back out into the cold night air. Taking their time, making sure it was safe, they slowly crept around the foundation of the building until they were in eye sight of the farmhouse. They planned to quickly run across the yard and old gravel driveway and run straight into the house. If anything saw them they would just have to use one of their many escape routes.

They all crouched down and got ready to spring from the relative safety of the shadows of the little out building. Prince was just about to whisper 'go' when off in the distance they heard a coyote howl, followed by the barking of dogs. They crouched even lower, their bellies firmly pressed against the cold snowy ground.

The cats listened to the commotion in the distance for a short time then decided, whatever was going on, it would be wise to hole up in the house. They scampered across the yard to the farmhouse and up onto the porch, Prince pausing a moment to look behind them and make sure they weren't followed. Soon they were all comfortably back in their little room on the big cushy bed looking out the window, watching intently for any signs of danger.

Chapter 15

The dogs had spent some time bedded down under the pines and it was late into the night when TW finally stood, shook off the snow, and roused the others. All of them had found a bit of restless sleep, except for Shep who'd spent the time watching and listening. Mostly he was watching TW.

The dogs groggily got to their feet, giving out a few tired yawns and shakes to wake themselves. They were all excited to finally be going back to the Den.

They were hardly yet fully awake when TW let them know they would be circling back to the cats. The cats would be out, cats hunt at night he told them, they could sneak up on them and surprise them, they'd never see it coming.

Fluff and Glodie comically dropped their jaws in disappointment at this news. Even Rat let out a little whimper but quickly shook it off, embarrassed at his behavior in front of his revered leader. Slow nearly cried.

Shep had no reaction whatsoever, he figured something was up as he'd been watching TW and observed that he never even tried to sleep. He had noticed that TW had been restless and fidgety the entire time the dogs had hidden amongst the pines. Shep was fully awake and standing off by himself as he usually did, thinking that this is the plan TW comes up with after hours in the cold, dark night? But Shep was tired and hungry and didn't feel like arguing, and he had no love for cats anyway. And besides, he was kind of curious to see how this obsession of TW's played out. He thought that maybe this could be the last straw and he could turn the pack against TW if things went badly.

TW ignored all of their whimpering and groans and set out straight away. He was surprised when he saw Shep trotting beside him. The shepherd had a steely look in his eyes and kept them focused on the path ahead. This made TW smile inside, maybe the shepherd was finally getting it, maybe he would be a good little doggy and follow his leader from now on.

It wasn't long and they could see the farm's silo above the trees, they were getting close and TW slowed his pace. He was determined and focused. They would get close enough to see the farmhouse, then they would stop and watch for any sign of the cats. If they saw them they'd give chase, if not they would slowly approach the farm yard and sneak about, hopefully catching the cats unawares.

While concentrating on the path ahead TW caught a familiar scent and soon after noticed a movement in the trees just off the road to his right. He remembered what the scent was at nearly the same time he heard the howl.

The same two coyotes from earlier emerged from the tree line, snarling viciously and staring the dogs down. TW, Shep and Rat all held their ground, the other three backed up a step or two. TW growled at them for this, quickly conveying to all three that their fate would be sealed if they didn't stand with him. They understood, now all six dogs faced the coyotes. The coyotes advanced.

The attack was sudden, the coyotes lunged in after the dogs, TW and Rat engaging one of the coyotes. The other grabbed Fluff in his jaws but before he could bite down he was hit full force in the flank by a charging Shep. The coyote went sprawling across the ground, tossing Fluff up in the air. She hit the ground hard and lay there motionless.

TW and Rat were having some success with the other coyote. The battle was vicious, their heads a blur as they snapped and tore at each other. TW took a bite to his right shoulder and yelped in pain. The coyote released him as Rat bit into his side and Goldie snuck up from behind grabbing his leg.

This was enough for the coyotes, they'd hoped the former pets would be good for a meal. They'd figured to kill one or two and chase the others off. However, the fight had become dangerous. They were both hurt, but not so badly that they wouldn't live to fight another day. The coyotes gathered themselves and snarling and snapping, backed away. Soon they turned and trotted into the trees. The dogs did not follow.

After the coyotes left, Shep went over to where Fluff lay, fearing the worst. He sniffed at her then licked her face a couple times. She opened her eyes and groaned.

She asked if they were gone in the way a dog might ask such a question, by looking this way and that, sniffing the air. Shep assured her that they had run them off. She smiled at this and stood on very shaky legs.

There was some blood on her back where the coyote had grabbed her. Shep and Rat licked at the wounds and determined they weren't too bad. Fluff had been lucky. If Shep's berserker charge had been a split second later the coyote would have fully bitten down and crushed the life out of Fluff. It had been a very close call.

After things settled down a bit TW was ready to head back to the farm. Shep, of course, was against this idea. Shep said nothing, he was encouraging Fluff to come with him. Fluff needed to head back to the Den and recover from her ordeal. With a look and a low murmur, somewhere between a growl and a sigh, Shep was encouraging the others to come with him.

The time was ripe, TW was injured, Shep was making his stand. Shep moved off with Fluff. TW growled at them and followed. The other three dogs watched. Slow and Goldie would be all for going with Shep, Rat was torn. He knew his friend Fluff needed to go back home and he was beginning to see how irrational TW was being. They were all very tired and very cold, this behavior was becoming more and more risky. All because of some stupid cats.

TW limped forward a few more steps, his front shoulder hurting him. Shep turned and growled viciously, it was the same growl that had given the coyotes pause. He appeared ready to explode into action.

Surprised by Shep's reaction TW just stood there, eyes wide, mouth agape. After a short standoff Shep turned back to Fluff and they started off, heading back to the Den. Goldie and Slow soon followed. Rat approached TW and with a small whimper asked him what he wanted to do. TW just stood there, watching his pack desert him, their figures quickly dwindling into nothingness, absorbed by the dark snowy night.

Rat's head was on a swivel, torn between TW and the rest of the pack. He tried to watch the pack go and look for any reaction from TW. TW, however, did not acknowledge Rat's presence in the slightest way. Rat gave one final short little whimper to announce his intentions and went scampering off into the night after Shep and the rest of the pack.

TW stood where he was, motionless, gazing out into darkness. He thought of nothing and simply stood still.

The snow was beginning to gather on his thick winter coat but he felt neither that nor the cold. He was slightly aware of the throbbing in his shoulder, numbed as it was by the cold, but it felt distant, almost if it were another's pain.

He stood for some time, he stood alone, and he gathered himself. It was cold, there wasn't even the hint of a breeze, and big fluffy flakes of snow were gently falling. There was hardly a sound. TW strained his ears, listening, he heard nothing. After a time he imagined he could hear the snow flakes strike the ground. He watched them, mesmerized. It was a gentle snow that fell, large flakes but spaced well apart, it could snow like this all night and probably add only an inch or two to the existing snow cover. But it would be enough to hide any animal paw prints. Soon, he thought, any tracks he found would be fresh.

He gave one last glance in the direction the pack had gone then turned and trotted off towards the farm. This was the night that he would finally take out those cats, he could feel it. He would deal with the pack and that meddlesome Shep later.

As he headed towards the farm his anger at Shep and the rest of the pack was building. He tried to shake it off, he wanted to focus on the cats, but try as he might he could not. That Shep, pretending once again to be a loyal follower, only to go his own way, ignoring his leader. TW was done with him. Shep would be gone and he didn't give a damn who got hurt or if the pack was broken up for good. Shep would be gone. Then, the other dogs, he would deal with them, they would all get in line or be gone too. He could get by on his own, he didn't need any of them. They needed him and yet off they had trotted with

Shep. Just as his anger began to consume him the farm came into view, shifting his focus.

He stopped, looking intently for any signs of movement in the yard ahead. He sniffed the air. There were faint scents of the day before, the coyotes, the dogs, and most of all, the cats. He sat on the path, he was in no hurry. All thoughts of the pack had vanished, he was focused, he was a hunter, and his prey was just ahead.

The Den wasn't far but it was an arduous journey. Fluff was in pain and moving slowly. The snow was causing her more difficulties than usual. She was dragging her feet through the snow with her head down as she went, not trotting along with her typical bounce. Shep led and had Rat go next with Fluff right behind him, in this way the two dogs made somewhat of a path for Fluff to follow.

Slow followed right behind Fluff, encouraging her as they went. Goldie took up the rear, often turning his head to check behind them, fearful that at any moment TW would come charging into view bent on taking revenge for their desertion, or that the coyotes would suddenly appear to ambush them in their weakened state. Fluff was the only one injured but they were all desperately tired and hungry. That and they were missing TW. Hate him if you will but he was strong and vicious, Goldie doubted the little pack could fight off the coyotes without him. They were as vulnerable as the pack had ever been.

After what seemed like much too long a time the pack reached the Den. Fluff plopped down in her favorite spot, a corner of the main room in which she and Rat had tucked a comfy blanket from one of the beds upstairs. Too tired to pay attention to pangs of hunger she immediately went to sleep.

The other dogs headed to the basement and drank out of puddles that had formed on the floor near a broken window and a leak in one of the walls. It seemed pretty common now to find water in basements. While taking turns at the water they spoke in tired whispers of the events of the night. Rat asked Goldie about Shep's charge that sent one of the coyotes sprawling, he'd missed this while battling with the other coyote. After hearing Goldie's rendition he looked at Shep in a whole new light. Rat admired this kind of toughness, maybe he'd been wrong about Shep.

There were fearful whispers from Slow who was concerned what TW would do once he showed up. To this several of the other dogs thought 'if', however none of them voiced their doubts. They were all much too tired to talk long and they soon left the basement. Back up stairs the dogs bedded down for what was left of the night. Looking for food would have to wait until the day.

Shep sat and looked them over, a very sad looking group they were. He would have rather they found a new place to call home but they were in no shape to go poking around deserted buildings in the middle of the night. He knew that if TW came back now he'd be on his own if it came to a fight, and he wasn't going to risk that. If TW forced his hand he would leave the pack and make his own way. As it was he figured that there would be a lot of posturing and TW would once again take over leadership of the pack. He sat still, watching and listening, as all the other dogs slept. Eventually after a long time of waiting for TW to appear, he curled up and with many thoughts swirling about in his tired brain, went to sleep.

As the rest of the pack was arriving back at the Den, TW was beginning his advance on the farm. It had stopped snowing and the night was very still. TW walked slowly over the fresh fallen snow, his steps nearly soundless except for a slight crunch when a paw would occasionally break into the couple of inches of firmer snow beneath the soft powder on top.

TW detected no movement. The scents of dog and coyote were from their first confrontation with the coyotes, nothing new there. The scent of cat was much fresher, they had been in the yard after the dogs had left. He walked forward and picked up the scent, fresh as it was he could nearly see the path the cats had taken from a nearby barn to the old farmhouse. He followed the path to the porch of the farmhouse. There he paused and looked over the house, leary of what might be lurking in the shadows.

He did not like houses and tried to avoid them. The Den was different, they had made a home out of it, but all other houses made him nervous. He suspected that they would find people in them, people who would leash him, lead him. He was the leader now, he did not want to be kenneled or tied up. He was free now, and the world was his. People would change that.

Pushing his fears away he went up the steps and noticed the ripped screen on the front door. The scent was strong here, there was also little tufts of cat hair on the screen. The conclusion was obvious, even to TW. This is where they were, where they called home. He'd found the cat den.

This must have been why Shep had been poking around the porch, he thought. TW had known the scent was strong here but his deep distrust and fear of houses had caused him to dismiss the house as a hiding place.

As he thought about this he knew he was being irrational and he should have probably listened to Shep, or at least explored this area with him. He'd never thought this way before, never had such doubts. He shook his head to clear it, bringing his focus back to the door in front of him.

The rip wasn't nearly big enough for him, and there was a second door, only slightly ajar, blocking his path. It would be easy for him to bound through the thin screen door, ripping the screen as he went, but the second door was a big, solid, wooden door, and he'd crash into that.

TW was tired and his shoulder was hurting him or he would have probably already went crashing into the doors, hell bent on finding the cats. That and nagging doubts were beginning to form in his tired brain. Shaking his head again, he sat down and stared at the doors. As he sat there his exhaustion finally caught up with him and he laid down, curling up with his back pressed against the outside door. He'd decided to wait for daytime, cats were trickier at night, they could see much better in the dark. Day would give him the advantage. He was so tired, so very tired. Soon he was deeply asleep.

Back at the Den the other dogs were dropping off to sleep at this very time. The cats, however, were wide awake. Prince had been on watch and had seen TW enter the yard and woke the others. They'd heard TW at the front door and expected him to, at any moment, explode into the house. They heard the door creak then nothing. After a time Prince crept down the steps and approached the door. He stood near the narrow opening of the inside door and caught sight of TW's back pressed up against the outside door. Soon he heard the rhythmic breathing of the dog, obviously sound asleep. Back up stairs he went, and informed the other cats of this new predicament.

Now what to do? There were many high places they could hide. Tall furniture would be too dangerous, the dog could knock them over. The kitchen cabinets, that was the best place. There was a space above the top cabinets the cats could jump up to, no way the dog could get them there. Although, once there, if the dog discovered them, there was no escape, it would become a waiting game.

Ava mentioned the basement, there were many shelves that were high enough to escape the dog. There was also the broken basement window. It was a small window with two panes, one of which had been broken out. Big enough for a cat to escape through but not a large dog. Prince thought about this and came up with a plan. They could hide on the shelving underneath the window. If the dog discovered them they could, if they had to, make an escape out the window.

Sasha brought up the trouble they'd be in if the other dogs showed up. The dogs could station one or two outside the broken window while the others attacked the shelving. This wasn't good, none of the cats wanted to take a chance of getting caught in such an awful trap.

It really came down to just two options, hide the best they could inside the house or leave the place and do it soon. If they stayed they knew that nasty dog sleeping at the door would tear the place apart once he woke. The other dogs would probably show up soon. They didn't understand why they weren't already there. But once they came the cats would be trapped, cornered, nowhere to go. The choice was obvious, although none of them wanted to, they had to leave. They would sneak down to the basement straight away and make their way out the small window.

Quickly, but very quietly, they went down to the basement. They had to pass near the front door on the way down the stairs to the first floor. The dog did not stir, he was still fast asleep. Soon they were in the basement, and working towards the window. The shelves were cluttered and it was with great caution that the cats jumped up from shelf to shelf. It was the skills that cats naturally possess that allowed them to make it to the window with hardly a creak or noise of any kind.

The three cats huddled at the broken window. Though the night was calm the cold night air slowly streamed in through the opening, chilling their little faces.

At the broken window they discussed which direction to go. Sasha and Ava's old neighborhood seemed the logical choice. It was close and they were very familiar with the area. They'd only had one run in with the dogs anywhere near the old home, and that seemed like such a long time ago. This, they hoped, would throw the dogs off somewhat.

Prince said that the big dog at the door had obviously been following their scent so they would need to take a longer, indirect path. They would double back a couple times, go in a wide semi-circle, and hopefully arrive at Sasha and Ava's old forever home well before dawn. This would give them time to find good hiding places and escape routes. They would have to move fast to get all of this done and find a safe place before the sun came up.

At Prince's urging out the window they went. They crept to the back of the house, very cautiously, feeling horribly exposed and vulnerable. Detecting no sounds or movements the cats quickly scampered from the back of the house to one of the outbuildings.

Ava said they should go inside, make the dogs think they were hiding within. This was a great idea, the cats ducked inside through a loose wall board. They moved about this way and that, leaving cat scent all over the small barn. Prince then led them up to a loft with a small windowless opening that had a short eve overhanging the back of the building.

They went outside, onto the short roof, their paws sinking in the cold snow. There was a large maple tree with branches that grew up over the eve, they easily climbed up onto one of the bigger branches, made their way over to the trunk of the tree then down into the field. This, they hoped, would throw the dog off their trail..

Off they went, the old farmhouse to their right, the old neighborhood also to their right but further on, past the farmhouse. It would be so nice to turn and head directly home but that wouldn't have been very wise, they would have to pass much too closely to where TW slept. They hurried through the field as best they could. The snow was firmer here and the cats were able to make good time. Weeds and tall grasses poked through snow here and there, providing them some cover.

Soon they came to a small creek, it was the very same creek they had used to rid themselves of fleas just a few short months ago. It seemed like the very distant past. This was an area they hadn't been before, it was a ways upstream. After taking a few minutes to catch their breath they started moving again.

They followed the stream, walking quickly but soundlessly along the bank. After a time they came to a bridge over the same road that separated their old neighborhood from the farm. Here they stopped for a short rest and to check their surroundings. They had been watching closely for any dog or other creature that might be following, none had been detected. Resting at the bridge they listened carefully, not a sound was heard. It was such a still night they all agreed that they could hear the crunching of old snow under heavy paws a mile away. They felt reasonably reassured that they weren't currently being followed.

When they set off again they elected to go under the bridge instead of risking being out in the open and crossing the road. It was slow going, the bank was very rocky. They had to pick their way carefully, stepping slowly from one cold slippery rock to another. They didn't want to risk walking on the ice covered stream as they'd noticed small patches of open water. They couldn't chance getting wet on a cold night like this, it would mean certain death. It wasn't long and they were back out in the moonlit night quickly walking along the bank of the creek.

They had followed the winding little stream for some time now, it had turned and twisted, taking them away from the farm. They heard nothing and felt reasonably safe. If they were threatened there was thick brush to hide in and tall trees to climb. Soon they arrived at a familiar spot, the very place Ava and Sasha had rid themselves of those pesky fleas a few short months ago. They stopped and told Prince.

This was where they would turn away from the stream and head back towards their old home. Dawn was still and hour or two away, the clouds had cleared and the moon was bright. It had gotten colder and the cats all longed for shelter. They headed up the bank and scurried along an old wooden fence row that was in poor repair. It wasn't long and they could see the houses of their old neighborhood. It lifted the spirits of both Sasha and Ava, and a little tiny feeling of homesickness stole over them.

The first place they stopped was their old home. The door was wide open now and it was very cold inside but it still reminded them painfully of home and comfortable days spent lounging in the sun with their loving family. A small tear appeared in the corner of Ava's eye, for a long time now she hadn't wanted to be an outdoor kitty and being home again made that feeling much worse.

She closed her eyes and for a moment could almost hear the voices of her humans, could almost feel their gentle hands petting her, the warmth of home washing over her. She felt like purring, but did not. Prince's mew's broke her thoughts.

He wanted them to move on. The dogs knew this place, didn't they? The cats weren't sure. They had lost the dogs here once before, hiding in a neighbor's house, but didn't know if the dogs had truly discovered their once forever home. There were plenty of other places to hide, why take the chance? They gave one last quick look around and, once again, left home.

The cats moved quickly down the winding street passing many houses that didn't seem like a good place for them. They settled on a nice home maybe a dozen houses away from their old place. It had a small broken window that they got to by climbing a tree that overhung a small porch roof. They surveyed the house and found it empty, and, more importantly, they found no other point of entry. They felt safe from prowling dogs here. It wasn't long and they had all curled up together, just as the dawn had begun to break in the south eastern sky.

Chapter 16

TW awoke to a briskly cold dawn, the sun already lighting up the morning sky. The sun was low and seemed too small, but he could still feel its warmth. There had been so many days of gray skies, it seemed such a long time since he had felt the sun's rays.

Waking to the sun helped his mood slightly, if it weren't for that he would have been nearly manic. He was cold, tired, hungry, thirsty and his shoulder wound ached. An ache which helped to mask other pains. He turned from the sun and examined the doors. Thirst and hunger would have to wait, well, maybe the hunger would be satisfied he thought in a sinisterly hopeful way.

He put his front paws up on the screen door, where the rip was, and poked his head in. He pushed his snout against the inner heavy wood door, it did not budge. He pushed a little harder and it gave a little. He backed up and came back at the screen door more aggressively, tearing at the screen with his front paws. The screen was now in tatters and he was able to lean through and push the inner door open far enough for him to be able to squeeze into the opening between the two doors. He was then able to muscle himself into the house. The heavy door had been wedged into a crumpled old rug but TW was able to push his way into the house, struggling through the opening. The old door closed a bit after he was in but he didn't worry about that, he was already frantically sniffing about, cat scent filling his nostrils, but where were they?

The scent was everywhere but strongest by the stairs, he followed them up. It was quickly apparent what room the cats had spent most of their time in. TW bounded in and immediately began tearing the room apart. Pillows and blankets went flying, furniture tumbled and crashed. TW ripped and bit at everything he could find, in a complete wild rage. He'd thought they were there, the scent had been so overwhelming. Finally he stopped, set on the old wood floor, and looked about. He was disappointed he hadn't found the cats but felt some satisfaction at discovering, and pretty much destroying, their hideout.

He soon became more aware of his physical needs. Exploring the house he found a puddle in the basement, clean water dripping in from melting snow near a crack in the foundation. He drank deeply and was refreshed.

As he drank the light from a broken window caught his eye. He went over to investigate, the scent of cat was strong here. He stood on his hind legs and put his front paws on the shelving under the window. The shelves were old and in disrepair and his weight caused them to tip and spill some of their contents on the floor. Old pots and pans, planters, tools, and other assorted forgotten household items came crashing down in a deafening crescendo. TW dodged the falling debris and scooted up the stairs momentarily frightened out of his wits. After living in such a quiet world for so long the noise from the basement had nearly sent him into a panic.

He stood at the top of the stairs and gathered himself. It took some time but he eventually calmed down and went back to exploring. He thought about the basement window, the cats' scent had been strong in that area, maybe they were near that window, but he couldn't bring himself to go back down into the basement. After finding nothing else of interest in the house he squeezed through the front door and began to exploring outside.

He was too hungry to continue the chase and spent some time looking around the farm yard for something, anything, to eat. He was just about to give up and head out into the fields to try and dig up some frozen crops when he found two half eaten dead rats just inside one of the small barns and wolfed them down, bones, fur, and all. After this he went back towards the house. Walking around the back of the house he found the broken basement window he'd noticed before. It was mostly hidden by snow and old bushes and he'd never have noticed it if he hadn't been looking for it. The scent of cat was strong.

Up closer to the window he saw the fresh tracks, quickly he turned to follow. The tracks led to a small out building, he went inside, the smell of cat was everywhere. But he couldn't find the cats, it was like they had disappeared. He went outside and circled the building, finding no more cat signs. He was beginning to get frustrated. He started to run about desperately sniffing at the ground. He nearly ran headlong into a large tree near the building and, mostly by accident, he once again picked up the cats trail at the base of the tree. He tracked them into a field that led to a small creek that bordered the farm. He trotted along, nose down, keeping the tracks in sight, and the smell, always there, making him wild.

He lost the tracks near the creek but was able to follow the scent along the bank. It was fresh and easy to follow. He had them now. He was moving fast, trying to be as quiet as possible, eager to catch the cats out in the open. Shortly he came up to a bridge over the creek. He followed the scent and came to a halt just before he went under the bridge. The bank was very rocky and, stepping on one, found them too slippery to get a footing.

He stepped out onto the ice. Carefully he walked ahead. It was dark under the bridge, he headed for the light ahead. There was a cracking sound, he tried to run. The ice gave way all at once and he found himself plunging into the terribly cold water.

It was deep here, and the current had hold of him. His feet quickly hit the soft, sandy bottom of the stream. He pushed off and immediately smacked his head on solid ice. The moving waters had pulled him downstream, away from the hole he'd made when he broke through. He held his breath and looked up, seeing only ice.

Further he went, letting the waters pull him away from the hole in the ice he'd made when he broke through. He couldn't see it anyway, no way he could make it back. He bumped his head again and again against the ice. The ice, a lid to his watery grave, he saw it clearly. He couldn't hold his breath much longer, starting to panic. Seeing stars, losing consciousness, he gave a push off the stream bed.

His head easily broke through a thin spot in the ice. Gasping, coughing, sputtering out water, he frantically flailed with his front paws at the ice, breaking the ice even further. He jumped, broke through, jumped again, suddenly finding himself on the bank. In his panic he hadn't comprehend that he was only a couple yards off shore. The ice had been thin here and he'd smashed it from the hole he'd come up through all the way to the bank.

He sat heavily on the bank and took a few moments to gather himself, calm down, let the panic subside. Taking a deep breath he stood and shook the excess water from his thick coat which was full of natural oils that kept the ice cold water from penetrating to his skin. A couple more shakes and he was ready to move on.

That had been a close one, TW thought. He'd been in too much of a hurry, too dead set on getting those cats to pay much attention to his surroundings. It had very nearly cost him his life. If he wouldn't have hit that thin spot right when he did, well, he knew he'd be dead right now, his body bumping along under the ice.

All because he had to chase those cats. Why, he asked himself. He shook again, refusing to answer, and picked up the scent. Starting after the cats he quickly found himself back in the shadow of the bridge. Without hesitation he climbed the bank and crossed over the road to the other side of the bridge, puzzled as to why he hadn't done that in the first place.

He picked up the cat scent as he crossed the road, and soon found cat tracks again. After a time the tracks led him up the bank. Soon he was following the scent along an old wooden fence. This led him to what looked like a deserted neighborhood. This was where the cats were hiding, one of these houses, he was sure of it.

He was able to follow the scent, and tracks which he'd once again found, to a large tree near a big white house in the middle of the subdivision. It was obvious the cats had climbed this tree but they were nowhere in sight. There were no tracks leading away and there were no leaves to hide them. He could tell they weren't in the tree, what was this, where had they gone? He was unable to reason out how the cats had just up and disappeared. He sat down to ponder.

Back at the den Shep awoke first, a dull morning light in his eyes. Pushing aside the drapes with his snout his eyes were dazzled by the morning sun that the window coverings had hidden. It felt good to see the sun, such a rare occurrence these past few months. They had slept late, the sun was already about two hours up in the southeastern sky.

More eastern now then south, it was coming home for the summer. The days were getting longer and the sun stronger as it came north, leaving the southern hemisphere to once again share its favor with the northern. Seeing it, feeling it, cheered Shep, and encouraged him. He went about rousing the other dogs, he had to speak with them and plan their next move.

After the dogs had drank some water and went outside to relieve themselves he gathered them back in the main room of the house. He let them know he was leaving, and leaving very soon. He had no idea what TW was up to or when he'd be back but he planned to be long gone by then. Today he would take to the fields, rooting around through the snow, digging up beans to eat. He'd make his way west, TW and the farm were to the east. He figured he would find another house to bed down at maybe just a couple miles away, then work further west the next day.

He told them they were all welcome to come with him. It might take a few days before they found a nice place and settled into a new permanent den but he wanted to make sure there was a good deal of distance between themselves and TW. He said he would be leaving soon. He gave the other dogs a minute to process this, then turned and slowly walked out into the front yard. He paused out on the snow covered sidewalk, feeling the warmth of the morning sun on his back, and turned to see the dogs already outside on the front porch, except for Rat whom, at that very moment, poked his head out the door and joined the family. Shep felt good, they all felt good, and off they went.

Rat had thought about going back to find TW, but he didn't dwell on this long. He had enjoyed his time being TW's number one, he'd felt powerful and with purpose. TW though, he was scary and becoming more erratic, and his pack wasn't like a family. It was dominance and intimidation. A family was caring and companionship. His new pack felt more like when his people family was his pack, and that is what had made him want to go with these dogs, they felt like a family.

He no longer wanted anything to do with power and purpose, he just wanted to live and enjoy life and those around him. Maybe, when the thaw came, he'd find a stream somewhere and sit and watch the water go by, no worries or cares, just be at peace. He used to go with walks with one of his humans and they'd do that, sit by the water and watch it flow. Something about the water, it just seemed to latch onto troubles and carry them away.

On this day he was thinking more about his people than he had in a long time. Oh, how he missed them, as a subtle nostalgia swept over him. The feelings, the memories, gently they caressed him, flowing over him like water, taking his cares away. He smiled to himself, let the memories of loss pass, and followed his new pack down the street.

Shep led them out behind the neighborhood, a farmer's field that he was quite familiar with butted up to it. They followed the edge of the field far to the west and near a fence row they started gleaning the field for beans. The snow wasn't as deep near the fence row, the trees and bushes acting as a natural windbreak, preventing the snow from drifting. This made bean digging much easier.

Many of the bean plants were poking up through the snow, others they dug for. It was easy pickin's and the dogs romped about, playing and having fun for the first time in a long time. This wouldn't be tolerated by TW. Shep was different, and he ran about with the others, enjoying the day. However, he often paused to look about with a wary eye. There were other things, besides TW, to fear in this new world they lived in. The other dogs took his example. They played, they ate, and they watched.

After a time they'd eaten a decent breakfast and decided to move on. They passed along the edge of another field, filled with tall stalks of corn. Here they all calmed down and became somewhat somber, who knew what lurked between the rows. They kept a wary eye on the corn stalks as they passed, picking up speed a little now. Today, this field, they did not like. Row after row of corn stalks made all that much more spooky by the quiet of a windless day. They all very nearly pissed themselves when the eerie quiet was suddenly broken by a rough sounding bean fart. Slow apologized, they all laughed, and continued on.

After the corn field they turned north, passed another empty field then turned west again. In this way they worked themselves away from the old den. It was afternoon and they came to a small neighborhood, just one road that jutted out into a farmer's field like a misplaced finger pointing south. There were only a dozen houses. They walked the length of the street and it seemed deserted. They found old deer tracks and little else. Even the scents were old. Shep had worried they would come across another dog pack in any neighborhood they might find, he'd figured there would be territorial issues when that happened. This place, however, was deserted. The sad fact was that this had been a hard winter for pets as it was the first winter most of them had had to fend for themselves. There were fewer, much fewer, house pets then there had been last fall.

Right on cue, as the pack walked between a couple of the houses, they came upon the remains of one of their own. It had been devoured, likely by coyotes, its bones were bared and gnawed. But it was old, the tracks were gone and the scent of coyote very very faint. It was likely this dog had lain here for months, long ago passing from starvation, then savaged by a passing coyote pack. This scene didn't inspire fear, only sadness, in the pack. They gazed upon their fallen comrade and wondered about him, did he live here? Did he, only a few short months ago, play with his forever family in this very yard?

They left and, after a time, down the street a bit and on the other side of the little road, found a house to call home. This house seemed the most comfortable, its basement had plenty of water, and, most importantly, there were two points of access. The front door was firmly shut but nearby there was an open window with the screen ripped out. The window was low to the ground, maybe less than two feet, and the snow had drifted up making a nice little ramp. Once the snow melted it would be hard for the small dogs and maybe Slow, but they could still use it in a pinch, especially as an emergency escape route. There was also a backdoor that was jammed open by snow and other debris that had blown in. This led to some stairs that went up one level to where the open window was. They found a nice cozy room away from the open window where they could bed down. They dragged blankets and pillows from other rooms and spent part of the afternoon making their beds. Then most of them settled in for a nap. Shep surveyed the scene, this was obviously going to be their new den. All the dogs had settled in quickly. It was fairly safe, and about as comfortable as they could expect.

Chapter 17

TW woke at the base of the tree where he'd tracked the cats to. He'd sniffed around the tree, looking this way and that, but there was no sign of them. He'd spent such a long time staring up into the big tree his neck ached. He just could not figure this out.

He was hungry and cold and could sit here by this old tree no longer. He gave one last quick look around, sniffed the air, which was still ripe with cat, and trotted off. The house by the big tree where he'd lost the cats seemed to have no way to get in, he started going house to house, checking for one he could gain access to. Maybe he'd get lucky, find and open door, and barging in, find the cats lounging in the living room, disturbed from their slumber by his presence. He'd make quick work of them. He began salivating at the prospect of this dream scenario. Or was it the people food he might find in open cupboards that made him hungry? He just did not know. He couldn't understand where his thoughts were leading him to.

He did find an open front door, and he did go barging in, but there were no cats. The place had been ransacked by other animals. Cupboards were opened, empty torn boxes were strewn, chairs were overturned, and nary a crumb did he find amongst the wreckage. The smell of rodent was strong, overpowering, the smell of larger wild animals was vague and distant.

Lots of homes, he'd learned over time, were like this. The bigger animals, raccoons, possums, had gained access and gone through the pantries. Some even lingered on, to sleep off their gorging with long winter naps. Afterwards the rodents had taken over. Soon, after a few litters had been born, the rodent populations had exploded, this tremendous population growth literally fueled by human leftovers. Many houses were like this, every last bite of human food had been devoured, leaving hundreds of hungry mice scavenging for nothing. Shoes and rugs, wooden door trim and wool sweaters, all kinds of odd things were chewed and gnawed upon. Then the mice began streaming from these homes, out into the cold on a desperate search for food. He'd seen their myriad of paths around many homes and their scent was everywhere.

This, of course, was great for cats. He'd seen quite a few glowing eyes peeking out of hiding places, and cats scampering up trees, but he rarely gave chase, they weren't his cats. Besides, cats weren't worth the effort now. Most had become quite feral and were too hard to chase. The field crops, the rodents, some homes that hadn't been taken over, there was plenty of easier ways to sustain himself. Now sustaining himself was a sideline, a small story beside a larger story, his blind ambition to get these cats. He'd never rest.

He'd never rest, no, that wasn't right. He'd find something to eat in one of these houses, he just knew it. Then he'd rest, find a comfy people chair, or bed, and nap long and hard. His thoughts were getting confused, he shook his mighty head, clearing it. Stop thinking, he thought.

Back at the house with the big old maple tree, Prince had set in an upstairs window, peering out and watching TW. He saw him arrive, saw him craning his stupid neck for what seemed like an hour, too dumb to figure out where the cats had gone. Vainly staring into the tree, probably hoping that if he just kept looking the cats would magically appear from wherever they'd gone. Prince watched as TW settled down for a nap, then saw him awake a short time later, watched as he'd finally trotted off down the street, thankfully, too dumb to ever look up and into the window where Prince sat.

Prince knew he'd taken a risk on that happening, but he'd hidden himself well and didn't think a casual glance in his direction would reveal his hiding place. He woke Sasha and Ava, the latter of which was already stirring. This was the first they heard about TW tracking them to this house. At first the news got them quite agitated but as Prince told the story, embellishing on occasion to add a little humor to TW's ineptness, they felt better. They especially liked the part about TW trotting off.

However, they all knew he wouldn't go far. During Prince's recounting Sasha had asked about the other dogs. Where were they? Why was TW alone? After some speculation they all, rightly, came to the same conclusion. At least they hoped they were right. TW's obsession had broken up the pack, what other explanation could there be?

The cats contemplated their next move. They preferred to stay here. Luckily it looked like they could, for a short time anyway. Like usual there was water in the basement. The house hadn't been ransacked as bad as some but the rodents had taken over at some point. They figured it was the second wave, rodents leaving houses gleaned completely of every last crumb, searching for a new place to call home, had stumbled across this one. They must have found small holes and cracks and worked their way in. The human food was gone now, but it hadn't been long. The cats had to work hard but they eventually tracked enough rodents to make a decent meal. They knew they'd have to leave this house at some point, for better hunting grounds. Hopefully not for a few days. Time enough for TW to wander off? That was their hope.

They were tired and even though the day was nearly over and night approached they decided to forgo their usual nightly prowls and head back up stairs to sleep. They cuddled together in a small room only a doorway away from the room with the open window. The house was comparatively warm, the day's sunshine temporarily chasing away the deep winter chill. They cared not to remember how many times they had tried to sleep in bone chilling cold. It may have been only a few degrees above freezing as they all drifted off to sleep, but it felt like a summer night to them. So they slept, deep and long, dreaming of the forever homes left in the past, a past seemingly so distant, and now, dreamy in of itself.

It was light out before the cats finally roused themselves from sleep. Of course they had woken now and then during the night, as cats often do. They'd give a wary look around, listen to the still of the night, then, once satisfied as to their safety, drift back to sleep.

They all felt very refreshed and spirits were high, nothing like a good night's sleep to improve one's outlook on life. They went down to the basement to drink from a puddle and then spent some time exploring the house. They were able to make a small meal of unwary rodents as they investigated. Some mice had probably spent their entire short lives inside one house, never facing a predator, this worked to the cats advantage. This house, however, had been emptied of food, and the mice that were left were thin and few. The cats knew they would have to leave this comfortable sanctuary to hunt, but they were content for this day, and in no hurry to venture outside where TW was undoubtedly lurking.

As for TW, he'd wandered about the neighborhood for some time yesterday, exploring a few of the open houses as he went. Luckily he found one relatively undisturbed home. Gaining access through a side door, that appeared to have only recently given way to months of shifting winter winds, he found a nice home with no scent of larger animals. The rodents had been there but the damage wasn't yet extensive. There was a pantry and he was able to jump up and knock some unopened boxes off an upper shelf. He dined delightfully on graham crackers and a bran and raisin cereal.

With a full belly TW had given in to sleep before the sun had even set. He found a nice older chair and settled in on its deep soft cushions, sleep quickly overcoming him. He'd woken once during the night, a vivid dream of his forever home, bounding up onto the sofa to greet one of his people, settling down on its soft cushions with his head in their lap. It felt so real.

It had taken him a little while to get his bearings as he looked around this unfamiliar deserted house. After a time the nostalgia faded and he fell back asleep. Deep and long he slept, waking just before the dawn. He drank from a toilet, ate some more cereal, relieved himself outside, then headed back to his comfy chair. Here he slept away most of the morning.

When he finally awoke the sun was well into the sky. He felt refreshed, a little sore here and there, but not bad. Nothing like a good night's sleep to improve one's outlook on life.

He must have been simply exhausted to have slept this long, too focused on those cats to take proper care of himself. The cats, that was the first time he'd thought of them, he'd felt so rested and his mood had improved so much that he'd somehow lost his anger and hatred of them. What anger? Why? He couldn't remember. He was unsure of why the cats had pushed themselves back to the front of his brain.

Once again he shook his big head to clear it. With his brain cleared of troublesome thoughts he started to feel lonely. He went outside, heading back to the house with the tree, hoping to pick up the cats trail again. Maybe he could talk with them, then he wouldn't feel so lonely. He shook his head, then shook it again. He didn't want to talk with cats, these were crazy thoughts. He walked down the sidewalk, shaking his head.

Back at the house where he'd lost the cats nothing had changed. He followed their scent to the tree in the front yard. Here the cats had obviously climbed the tree but he'd lost them. The tree was barren of leaves but, once again, he sat at its base and gazed determinedly up at its empty branches. He looked over every branch and found no cats clinging to them, only one forlorn brown and twisted leaf, the single holdover from an impressive green canopy displayed by the large tree during the summer months.

TW stared at it and wondered how one leaf could cling so desperately to its perch when all others had long ago succumbed to the strong winter winds. Then he thought to himself, I am like that leaf, clinging to these cats like the leaf clings to its branch. When all others have fallen, I yet remain, but to what end? There was yet no sign of spring buds. Soon they would come, and the last little leaf would surely then be pushed unceremoniously off of its branch, carried by the wind to some unknown destination.

Maybe it was too afraid of where it would end up to let itself go. Did it not realize it had no control over its fate? That fate would take it where it would. Calmly, or kicking and screaming, that was its only choice. TW thought that it would be hard to enjoy the ride if you were so worried about the destination that you could not let go of what little you had, even though that which you had was so precariously held that, regardless of your actions, it could be taken from you in an instant, by a chance gust of wind. Let go little one, TW thought, let go.

Was that me? Am I like that leaf? TW sat long and pondered, his neck soon stiff from staring up into the empty branches of the large tree so gloomily silhouetted by the gray winter skies. He'd lost his pack because of his obsession with the cats. He'd nearly lost his life, more then once, messing around with coyotes and falling through the ice. Now he sat, alone, and although filled with crackers and cereal, feeling empty just the same.

He began to miss the comradery of the pack, the sense of adventure that came with shared experiences. He had not treated them well. He'd been sometimes cruel, mostly just obstinate and full of himself. He'd enjoyed being the leader, but why? Just so he could impose his will on others? A leader should lead for the good of all, not just to fill some foolish internal need.

Overwhelming were his feelings, he no longer wished to dominate and control, he longed for companions and belonging. Maybe he should go and find them, make amends, follow if need be. Whatever it took to once again belong, to find brotherhood, to enjoy the gift of life instead of continually striving for more than it was meant to be.

Maybe it was the dream the night before, feeling safe, warm, with his family that caused him to feel this way. He remembered when he woke from the dream last night. He'd felt so at peace, so happy and content, so at home. Then the dream faded and he realized where he was. It was like a giant wave of sadness and longing for the past had washed over him. He sat there, under that tree, with the saddest face a doggie could muster.

Why were these cats so important, he thought. He could find easier meals. Was it that they'd made him look so foolish that day, so long ago, when he'd first spied them down at the creek? Or was it that they had eluded him for so long? Or was it just that they were cats and cats and dogs weren't supposed to get along?

He remembered, vividly, his forever home. The older cat that also lived there, sunning itself on the dining room floor by the slider to the deck, its favorite spot. So relaxed and serene the old chap seemed to be.

They'd spoken on occasion, shared a moment here and there. They were never really close but there was no animosity. He wondered what had happen to the old cat? He'd left the home, and the cat, shortly after the people had gone, never to return. Now, here he was, looking so desperately for cats that he had no reason to hate, no real reason to even be looking for, and now, it occurred to him, there was no reason to be here.

His head was spinning, this was a lifetime of thinking crammed into one moment, sitting under this tree. Once again, he looked up, and, at that moment, a gust of wind came along. The little leaf was grabbed by the breeze and pulled from its perch. But it wasn't that strong of a gust, surely there had been many more much stronger winds this long winter. Did it finally realize it was time and just let go?

TW watched as the wind carried the little leaf, twisting and turning in its swirl. It settled briefly on the porch roof of the big white house, the house it had helped shade only a few short months ago. As TW watched the leaf he caught the eye of a cat in the window right above the porch. They stared, returning each others gaze, nary a blink. It was that long haired cat, black ears, legs, tail, face, tan everywhere else. The companion of the tiger cat he'd nearly caught at the creek.

TW looked at the cat and noticed it had the most beautiful blue eyes. It was a beautiful creature, beautiful for a cat anyway. Its long fluffy fur, big bushy tail, how had it kept itself so well groomed?

The cat, he thought, once had a forever home, just like him. It had people that loved it, just like he'd had. He felt such overpowering homesickness that he had to lay down on the snowy ground. He'd not felt like this before, never had he let himself once feel so much despair at a past lost. And now it came all at once, overwhelming him.

He looked back up at the cat still watching him closely. He took a deep breath, exhaled, and smiled a sad, apologetic smile up at the cat. At that moment he broke free of all that had been holding him, let go of all his hate and anger, and a great peace enveloped him. He stood, gave the cat a kind and gentle smile, a slight nod of the head, turned and trotted off.

It felt good to be at peace, to let his troubles go. He wanted his friends, he hoped he could find them. He hoped they would take him back.

Sasha watched him go, a long time she sat watching the dog trot right down the middle of the street, until the big dog disappeared around a bend in the road. She went and found Prince and Ava and told them what she'd seen. They both thought it was probably a trick but Sasha was convinced it was not.

She attempted to explain the feelings she'd had as the dog had smiled and nodded then turned and trotted off. She was sure he'd left them, had left behind all of his consuming passion to bring about their demise. It was the look he'd given her, she told the other cats, that told her the dog was moving on. Something profound had occurred to the dog and he was gone, gone to follow some other path, carried away from them like a leaf on a gust of wind.

Chapter 18

At the new den Shep and the other dogs had settled in quite nicely. Over the next few days they had explored all the other houses in the neighborhood. At least the ones they could gain access too. They had discovered which nearby fields were worth foraging in. They had made small improvements to their new den, mostly with the bedding, a very important thing. They were all quite content.

A routine had been established, up early in the mornings they would forage house or field for breakfast, then they would go exploring. After checking out all the houses and the bordering fields they began to widen their arc, working further and further out from the home base.

They found a few older houses along the main road, spaced far apart, that were abandoned and thoroughly ransacked. They met a couple cats here and there, living on their own, living off the land. The dogs tried not to threaten the cats in any way, they reminded them of long lost forever homes as each dog, at one time or another, had shared a home with one or more cats. In this way they were kindred spirits. However, after many months on their own, the cats were wary and did not approach the dogs. They seemed too wary, thought Shep. By their actions the cats told the dogs what they already knew, there were no people, nothing had changed, they were still all on their own.

After about a week of exploring the dogs were trotting down a paved road and noticed another small neighborhood far up ahead. With keen eye sight they could see the houses, very small in the distance. Like their own neighborhood, this one was carved out of the farmers fields with nothing else around. They could be there in a quarter hour if they made good time. It was early so they decided to trot over and check out a house or two before heading back home.

Soon they passed another old abandoned farmhouse, set close to the main road, a paved road that had surely been busy at one time, before the people had gone. As they passed the house they saw a blur of gray as something scurried from the bushes up onto the porch of the old house.

Shep spoke, who goes there, he'd asked. A cat replied in a nervous voice, asking the dogs to just keep moving and leave him alone. In animal speak Shep told the cat that he had nothing to fear from them, they were just exploring the area. The cat, still quite nervous, again asked the dogs to leave him alone. Goldie asked the cat if he'd seen any people, thinking that a change of subject might help the cat relax, which it did, a little anyway. The cat quickly said no but, in a hopeful tone, asked if the dogs had seen any, which, of course, they had not.

In a dejected voice the cat mumbled some inaudible reply and slunk further into the shadows of the porch. Slow told the cat they'd keep moving but again reassured him that he had nothing to fear from the dogs. Slow told him that all of them had once shared a forever home with people and a cat, some more then one, and that they had met many cats during their adventures and none had come to any harm.

This seemed to reassure the cat and he inched forward a little so that the dogs could see his bright green eyes, gray matted fur and nervous twitching ears. The cat spoke quickly, he did notice something different about them, the other dogs he'd meet would have not spoken to him, only chased, wanting to hurt, wanting to kill.

He warned the dogs, they should turn around. There were other dogs up ahead, not nice dogs, mean dogs. These dogs lived a long way off but on occasion they foraged out this far. They had tried to catch him but he'd hid, for days he'd hid. He got so hungry, so thirsty, so cold, so tired. But they left, and now he was wary, always waiting for them to come back, always afraid.

He'd thought of leaving, heading in the direction that Shep and his friends had come from, to get further away from the mean dogs. But this was his forever home, he didn't want to leave, he wanted to wait for his people, maybe they would come home soon. So he found hiding places, he worked out escape routes, he watched, and he waited.

Shep had asked the cat how many dogs were in the other pack, but the cat didn't know. He would only say that he'd seen a couple at a time and once the dogs had spoken to him and told him they were part of a large pack and they'd be back, back to get him. He'd been so frightened.

For a time the dogs stayed and chatted with the nervous little gray kitty. He seemed very thankful to have someone to talk to that wasn't trying to eat him. They talked about their humans and wondered when, or if, they'd be back. The spoke about the weather and how it seemed winter was ending. It was a friendly time, so rare in a ruthless world.

After they ran out of things to say the dogs thanked him for his warning and off he went, to hid in one of his hiding places. Despite the gray cats' warning the pack still wanted to check out the other neighborhood, even if it was only a quick look around. There was no scent of other dogs, they hadn't been this way in a long time. So the dogs trotted forward.

At the new neighborhood they finally caught dog scent. It was a few weeks old but there had been many. They identified ten different dog scents but there was no way to know if these were all part of the same pack. They checked out a few houses but finally got nervous and left. There was nothing here that they needed, or even wanted. They wouldn't come this far in this direction again.

The pack trotted past the farmhouse with the gray cat, turned and headed out into the fields, they would eat some more beans as they went. From an opening high up in a big old barn the gray cat watched them go. He watched for a long time, he liked those dogs and hoped maybe he'd see them again.

It was late afternoon before they arrived back at the Den. Once inside they quickly settled in, getting a drink, doing some grooming, and chatting about the days adventures.

This was something they all enjoyed, relaxing together, as the sun set on another day, and talking about the day they had just experienced. They were all having the time of their lives, it was the first time since losing their people that they were enjoying life. Their coats were thick and the weather, though cold, had not been miserable. They were fed well enough, and they were all healthy. Fluff had long since healed from her coyote wounds.

They always seemed to find enough to eat. The exploring was enjoyable. The comradery was the best thing of all. Shep was a great pack leader. He kept them safe, was always rational and reasonable, guided their daily adventures, and seemed to enjoy the pack's company as much as they enjoyed him. Rat would easily admit, if anyone cared to ask, that Shep was a much better leader than TW.

The dogs all speculated about what had happened to TW. This was often a topic of conversation. It had been several weeks since they last saw him. All of the dogs, especially Shep, had expected him to track them down by now, resulting in a nasty confrontation.

Every day that went by without TW showing up seemed to lighten the pack's overall mood. Slow had been very nervous at first. It seemed too good to be true, and he found it hard to enjoy himself like the others. He was always watching, always waiting, for TW to return. He'd even had dreams, no, nightmares, of TW coming back.

It took a few days for him to put TW mostly out of his mind. Soon he joined the pack, running through the fields, barking and playing. He felt like a much younger dog. If you saw him scamper about you'd have thought of a dog that had never had much freedom suddenly being let loose to run and play in a wide open area. Seeing dogs so happy would erase any doubt anyone could ever have of dogs not having emotions. Maybe not as developed as people, but just as wonderful to observe.

This night, as the pack lounged at the Den, TW came back into Slows mind and he wondered aloud what had happened to him. Rat figured he was still after the cats, reasoning that he hadn't caught them or he'd have shown up here by now. Slow mentioned that maybe he'd been injured and/or the coyotes had caught up to him. Being without a pack would not be good in a situation like that. Shep expressed the possibility that TW had gone off in another direction and either joined or started a new pack. He, along with all the others, hoped that whatever was going on with TW that they had seen the last of him.

It had been several weeks, three, four, they didn't know, but it seemed like forever, like a lifetime ago since they'd left TW. The long trek home after the fight with the coyotes. The worry over Fluff and her injuries, which she was over now. The finding of, and settling in, at the new Den. All of the daily adventures since. Yes, it seemed so long ago, but yet they couldn't get TW out of their thoughts. What was he doing? Where had he gone? Was he going to enter their lives again? A worry that all of them had. Little did they know that by now TW had had his little epiphany, a change of heart, and had left his obsession, and his pursuit, of the cats.

After leaving the cats TW had made his way back to the old den. He foraged and took care of himself well enough, but he was a sad and lonely dog.

The familiar scents of the den quickly brought up memories of his friends. He'd wondered if they could ever take him back. He thought of all the things he'd done, the trouble and pain he'd caused, and he doubted it.

Still, he often found himself daydreaming of a reunion where he'd apologize profusely, tell them about his change, and they'd welcome him back. He'd gladly let Shep lead them, he just wanted to be part of the pack. Then reality would come back and sad thoughts of rejection would run through his head.

He knew well enough which direction they'd gone, he had found their tracks, smelled their scent. They must have left the den shortly after they'd left him as all signs were getting old.

He'd followed their path a short distance on more then one occasion, starting out with hopeful thoughts of reunion, turning back when thoughts of rejection would swim into his head. His emotions flip flopping so quickly made him question whether he was losing his mind. What must other animals think, watching him bound down a trail, head and tail up, an alert and excited look on his face. Only to shortly see him come back the other way, tail and head down, slowly walking a sad, sad walk. What a strange sight he must be.

He thought about how quickly the dogs must have left the old den. Even with the little dog's injuries, that's how desperate they'd been to get some distance between themselves and him.

This was how he spent the next few days, foraging and napping, all the while alternating between hope and despair. He would settle down at night and, before drifting off to sleep, tell himself that tomorrow would be the day. The day he'd not turn back. The day he would seek out his old friends.

Time was passing, as it always does, but at such a relative pace. For TW it dragged, the days painful as he wrestled with his troubled mind. For the pack the days flew by, busy and full of fun. If the dogs had a calendar they would have seen that the month had changed from February to March.

The days were getting longer, this they noticed, and it seemed to be warming up some. Warming up when compared to the bitter cold of deep winter. The sun did feel warmer on their backs, the days that it shined at least. As the sun set on another day, Shep, Fluff, Rat, Goldie, and Slow all settled in at the new Den and drifted off into a comfortable and contented sleep. At the old denTW fell slowly into a troubled sleep, full of painful dreams, and a cold loneliness.

It was early March, and each day the sun reached higher in the sky. The nights were still cold but the days were becoming much more bearable. The cats, with their winter coats, a thick fur that only Prince and, to a lesser extent Sasha, having been outdoor kitties, had experienced before, were comfortable on their nightly hunts.

There had been no threats recently, ever since TW had left. They were still wary and only left the house at night, but found hunting much more enjoyable when they weren't so often the hunted and weren't so often freezing half to death.

Sasha, Ava, and Prince had settled into their new home, the same one TW had tracked them to, with the big tree in the front yard overhanging the porch. Here they felt very safe, no coyotes or dogs were going to climb a big tree to gain access and there was no other way into the house. They were well fed, the nightly hunts always very successful. The days they spent lounging, napping, grooming, and for the first time in such a very long time they all found themselves, on occasion, almost too warm.

The sun would warm the house all day long and by mid afternoon, with their thick coats, they would find themselves almost toasty. Yes, the homes had never been this cold when the people were there, but yet, with such thick fur, they were as warm as the cats could ever want. They weren't complaining, not at all, it was such a welcome change that they enjoyed very much.

A week passed, then another. They watched as some of the snow began to melt away. Even a small patch of grass was exposed. Climbing the tree one morning, Ava noticed there were buds on the branches, yet another sign of a glorious spring to come.

Even though March was passing quickly by, some years winter would not give way to spring without a fight. This year old man winter, who could be a rotten old coot, struck back late one night.

The cats were leaving a nearby house, bellies full after another successful hunt. It had been snowing when they entered the house a couple hours earlier, only flurries, gentle fluffy flakes, the kind kids loved to catch on their tongues. Such a pretty little dusting of snow that made one think of Christmas time.

Now, when they were making their way back outside, they could hardly see. There were so many of the big flakes that they seemed to all be connected as they floated slowly and gently down to the ground. It was as if a waterfall had been magically turned to snow flakes, all the droplets suddenly puffing themselves out into beautiful crystals of ice, slowing and expanding out to cover the landscape. You could see through this snow about as well as you could see through a waterfall, nothing but shadowy shapes in the distance.

The cats made it outside, the snow was already so deep that they had to plow a path with their little bodies. Quickly the snow settled on their fur. It looked like some child had made three little snowcats instead of snowmen, except that these snowcats were moving. Slowly. A trip that only took them a couple minutes earlier that night took them nearly an hour. With great effort they fought their way home.

They climbed the tree with great difficulty, nearly blinded by the snow that was hitting them directly in the face as they went up. It was slow going as they inched their way along the big branch that overhung the porch.

Prince led the way, ploughing the snow off the branch as he went. He slipped once and nearly fell, digging in with all his claws just in time. At the porch they all jumped into deep snow and quickly bounded through the open window. They shook off the snow and groomed themselves then settled in to watch the storm from a window across the hall in the bedroom they had made their own.

The snow fell like this the rest of the night, so deep the cats wondered if they would be able to get out of the house. Once outside how would they get anywhere, how would they hunt? Maybe they should have stayed at the house they were hunting in, but it was unfamiliar and they often sought out the familiar. It comforted them.

As the sky began to lighten with the dawn, the snowfall lightened with it. When they could see a little better they were even more disheartened. More than a foot of snow had fallen, everything was covered. If their future wasn't now so much more scary it would have been beautiful to behold. A real winter wonderland. One can only take so much winter wonderland.

After a time they all sadly slunk away from the window and bedded down to sleep the day away, utterly exhausted from the night's adventure. They slept long and soundly, tired not only from the night's hunting and efforts to get home, but from the emotional toll of the added stress brought on by this late winter storm.

Chapter 19

As the cats were drifting off to sleep Shep and the rest of the pack were nervously watching the snow pile up outside the new Den. They hadn't been able to go on their daily adventure yet, having woke to already deep snow. They were barely able to push through the piles to go outside and pee in the snow. Fluff and Rat noticed, not so pleasantly, how hard it was to pee in snow deeper then you are. Then there was the problem of food, how would they be able to get through all this snow to the beans and corn in the nearby fields?

In the kitchen there was a cupboard with the door slightly open that contained a treasure trove of crackers, cereals, and other boxed people food. Out of the reach of rodents and other critters it had sat there undisturbed. The dogs had known it was there but they hadn't needed it, and besides it was too high up and they had not worked out any way to get at the food. With their bellies rumbling, one by one they made their way into the kitchen at sat looking longingly up at the boxes of food.

They were all getting quite discouraged as there seemed to be no way to get at all this wonderful food. It was like some kind of cruel joke, empty bellies with so much food just out of reach.

Suddenly Slow sat up straight, his ears perking up like a dogs will when they hear a noise such as a knock on the door or the sound of the mailman's truck. He barked at the other dogs, communicating quickly that they needed to get all the cushions and pillows and pile them up in front of this cupboard. This task they took to enthusiastically. Dogs were running and jumping all about, cushions off couches and chairs, pillows from beds, blankets and anything soft they could find, all this they brought to the kitchen. It was all great fun, even with empty bellies. They made a great pile.

The dogs all took turns trying to climb the soft little mountain but cushions would shift, pillows would fall, and dogs would tumble about this way and that. They hooted and hollered encouragement to each other, barking out gales of laughter as one after another fell head over heels. It was a great time, the falls were short and full of fun as they bounced off all the padding.

After a time, a fairly long time, as the dogs so enjoyed having fun that they kept up this mountain climbing for the rest of the morning and on into afternoon, they settled down and became more aware of their hunger. Shep took charge at this point, like he often did when the fooling around had run its course. He placed Slow on one side of the pile and Goldie on the other. They would do their best to keep the pile from shifting. He then worked his way up on top of the pile, crawling on his belly, wobbling and swaying as he went. He had Rat follow him. Shep then had Rat climb on his back. Shep stood up as quickly as he could and Rat launched himself at the cupboard. The door wasn't open enough and he slammed into it and went crashing down, taking Shep and most of the pile with him.

There was a shocked silence. Then, once everyone realized nobody was hurt, there was a deafening outburst of barking laughter.

One thing was accomplished by this unsuccessful attempt. After Rat had slammed into the cupboard door it had rebounded with the force of the blow and was now wide open.

It took two more tries but soon Rat was standing inside the cupboard and gayily launching box after box down upon his friends. He emptied the entire cupboard then flew down to a bouncy landing on the cushion pile to join the pack in a well deserved feast.

Back at the old den TW stood in the front yard, snow up to his belly, gazing in the direction he knew his friends had gone. He should have gone yesterday, he couldn't today. He'd started but the snow held him back, or so he told himself. For a time he'd continued to look hopefully off into the distance. He thought, he daydreamed, maybe one of them would come for him, bouncing through the snow, barking for TW to come join them, barking to let him know all is forgiven, barking for him to follow and that everything would be okay.

Soon he began to shiver. Sadly he dropped his hopeful gaze and turned back, ploughing his way through the fresh soft snow which glistened brightly in the morning sun.

Far from TW, on past the new den where Shep and his friends now lived, there was a farmhouse where a nervous gray kitty with bright green eyes lived. He had visitors the day before the storm. A large pack of dogs. He hid high up in a barn. The dogs knew he was there but could not see him and could not get to him. He had met a couple of them before, they had scouted the farm and chased him, given him quite the scare, but he knew the farm well and had eluded them.

It was a long time before the heavy snows would start to fall and the leader of the dogs, a big, light brown, mixed bread, with keen dark brown eyes and a very strong looking jaw, spoke with the cat. He told him that they wanted nothing to do with this old farm, there was nothing here for them, and one cat would barely make a decent meal for one of them. They would move on and leave him be if he would answer their questions. The dogs got scent of another dog pack in the nearby neighborhood and followed the scent here. They wanted to know everything the cat knew, what he had seen. The big dog warned that they'd know if he was lying, and if he lied to them then the pack would never rest till they got vengeance.

The big dog was very threatening, and the poor nervous little gray cat knew he meant what he said. He counted six dogs. They were all big, mean looking dogs, and scared him terribly.

This pack didn't let small fluffy dogs or older friendly dogs join, only big mean dogs. He knew he had to say something but he wanted to defend the other dogs, he felt bad for them as he knew there was no way they could protect themselves from these dogs. Little fluffy dogs and old dogs and friendly dogs, they couldn't hope to stand against this pack of big mean dogs.

So he told them a story. Yes, other dogs had come through here, they were mean and threatening so he'd hid. They found his hiding place and spoke with him, like this pack was now doing. There were five of them, (he knew this pack would know that from their scents, no use trying to hide this fact), and they were from a long ways off. They had journeyed far and were turning back and would never be here again. For dramatic effect he went on to say that the other pack told him he was lucky that they lived so far away and it wouldn't be worth traveling many days to hunt a scrawny little cat, and so they had left and that was the last he'd seen of them.

The big dog had laughed at this and said it didn't matter how far away these other dogs lived. They had entered their territory and this would not do. The pack would sleep here tonight, sarcastically thanking the cat for his hospitality, and hunt the other dogs in the morning. The gray cat did not like how the dog used the word 'hunt'.

The dogs took over the cats little home, they broke the front door and made a mess out of the inside. He could hear them barking and breaking things from his perch in the barn. It was dark before they settled down.

He was able to watch the house through a crack in the barn wall, they were all in there and, from how quiet it had become, apparently all sleeping. He'd worried that at least one of them would be on watch and be prowling around the barnyard. He made his way down to the floor and snuck out the back of the barn.

As he worked his way away from the house he always kept a hiding place near. From building to building he slunk and snuck. When he was at the last little building, far away from the house, he sat and watched and listened for a minute. Once he was satisfied there was no danger he quickly took to the fields behind the farm. It had began to lightly snow as he made his way, going in the direction he'd seen the friendly dogs go a few weeks past.

The gray kitty with the bright green eyes made good time as he headed off to find his friends. This was a big adventure, the biggest he'd ever been on. Before his people had gone he'd hardly ever left the little old farmhouse.

He'd been an indoor kitty for as long as he could remember, taken in by an older human couple when he was very young. He loved his people, he would often nap in one lap or the other while they would gently stroke his fur and scratch behind his ears. Now they were gone.

Even after they had left he'd still never wanted to leave the little house, but was finally driven out by hunger. Then he learned to hunt the barns, but he still spent his days in the old house, the only home he'd ever known. He questioned if he could ever call it home again, the dog pack had made a mess of it and now that they had violated his territory he wondered if he'd ever feel safe in the house again.

He put those thoughts behind him along with lots of distance. He skirted along the edge of a big field, cut diagonally through another and wound up on the shoulder of the road his old farmhouse was on. He ran along the side of the road for some time. He paused under a large oak tree and noticed that he was now leaving a trail of tiny cat footprints, the snow had begun to accumulate. He looked and listened and noticed nothing. He climbed up in the big tree, there were no leaves to obscure his view and he was able to see a long ways in all directions. He could see his home, small in the distance. He saw no signs of movement there, or anywhere else for that matter. Shortly he climbed back down and continued his adventure.

He left the road to run along the edge of another big field. Just as he'd began to worry that he was going the wrong way he came upon the scent of the small pack. They'd all pee'd on a small tree, or the nearby ground, at the corner of four fields. He briefly puzzled as to why dogs always had to pee in the same place, it seemed foolish to give away your location like that. He'd learned to bury his waste, deeply, so that none could use it to trace him.

He was able to determine their direction from here as the dogs had obviously been running about on the edge of these fields. The ground had been torn up by playing dogs and the cat could follow the path even as the snow had begun to cover the ground.

More and more snow fell, making travel increasingly difficult. Eventually the gray cat made his way to a small neighborhood, he went in the first house he found. Luckily there was a small enough opening in a broken side door for him to slip in. He was glad to be inside, the snow had really begun to come down and he'd had to jump over and push through the snow as it piled up. He wouldn't have been able to go much further that night.

The house had come into view just as he'd began to despair that he would be trapped outside in this terrible storm. He was desperately looking for a place to take shelter, some bushes or evergreen trees, when the house had suddenly loomed up before him like a great wall. He'd been momentarily shocked and slunk low in the snow, as if to hide from this large apparition in front of him. Quickly he realized it was only a house and scolded himself for his foolish, fearful reaction. Normally he could see well at night but it was very dark and the snow was so terribly thick that he could only see a few feet in front of him, otherwise a house would have never snuck up on him.

He was exhausted once he got inside but quickly regained a second wind when he heard the scurrying of rodents. He was a really good hunter now and soon had a decent meal. Afterwards he explored the house and found a comfortable hiding place, way up in a linen closet that had been left open. He was soon sleeping soundly, the first leg of his great adventure in the books.

Long did he sleep, so tired from his journey and the emotional toll of dealing with the mean dogs and leaving home. It was afternoon before he finally jumped down out of the closet. He looked out the doorway he'd used to enter the house and was amazed at the depth of snow. The air coming in wasn't as cold as you'd think and a large puddle of melted snow had formed on the tile floor in the entryway. He drank deeply, the water was cold and very refreshing.

After this he worked his way outside, struggling mightily through the snow, and found a place to relieve himself. He turned and was stunned to see the door was only a couple feet away from him. That was that, he was snowbound. It had taken tremendous effort to struggle through the snow just to go a few feet, there was no way he'd be venturing out to find the dogs today. At least they wouldn't have anything to fear from the other pack, he was sure they wouldn't be able to go anywhere today either. Although reassured that they'd be stuck at his old house and wouldn't be able to trouble him today, he was also saddened that the place he'd called home for so long would be further desecrated by a pack of dogs now snowbound and unable to leave.

Back inside the house he found the rodent population to be quite sizable and it wasn't long before he'd successfully fed himself. Still a little tired he settled back into his cosy little linen closet for an afternoon nap. This was about the same time as his dog friends were finishing up their afternoon meal after finally cleaning out the cupboard they'd spent half the day working on. The gray kitty suspected his friends were nearby, somewhere in this neighborhood, call it cat intuition. Or maybe it was that he'd thought he heard dogs barking in his dreams as he'd slept the morning away. He thought he'd woken once or twice to what sounded almost like dogs laughing but the sound was very faint and he'd been so very tired and slept so deeply he couldn't be sure. And dogs don't laugh, do they?

About this time Prince, Sasha, and Ava where making do with the few scrawny rodents they could find. They really liked their house, it made them feel secure, but it wasn't a great place to be snowbound.

Meanwhile TW had resigned himself to going hungry and he did his best to sleep away the day at the old den. Lots of snow had come in through an open window and melted on the floor, he did his best to compensate for his hunger by drinking plenty of water.

The same kind of scenario was playing out at the gray kitties old house as the mean dog pack was also snowbound and hungry. They argued and fought amongst themselves as a way to try and ignore their hunger, maybe not as healthy of a plan as TW's.

Later that afternoon all of the former pets noticed that it had warmed up significantly outside and the massive amounts of snow that had fallen the night before were already beginning to melt. It was getting on towards late March and in Michigan the weather could change quickly at this time of year.

To TW this meant that soon he'd be able to resume his daily debate and ask himself the question he asked everyday. Should I go find my friends today or not?

The gray kitty thought, if the snow continues to melt tomorrow, maybe he'd be able to get outside and explore and find out if it really was his friends he'd heard barking. The more he thought about it the more he was sure the sounds he'd heard came from familier dogs, but he'd be careful so as not to stumble upon another pack that might not be so friendly.

Prince, Sasha, and Ava were also hopeful of more snow melt. They knew they could sustain themselves for some time with just water, they had done it before, and there were a few more rodents in the house they could hunt, but they didn't like the idea of being hungry for days, not at all.

Since their humans had gone they had all experienced hunger, all the cats, all the dogs, and, of course, none of them liked this. The specter of prolonged hunger made the three cats very nervous. They hoped with all the hope former pets could muster that tomorrow would also be warm.

To the mean pack the melting snow meant they also could avoid going hungry. To their leader, who was itching for a fight, it meant that they could go looking for the pack that had invaded their territory a little sooner. He hoped they would be able to get going soon, the bickering and arguing was getting worse. The fighting would be amongst themselves if they were trapped here much longer.

All of the former pets watched as the sun set on another day, all hopeful, for various reasons, for a better day ahead. Would the weather continue to be warm enough to keep melting the snow? This was the question all the cats and dogs were asking themselves as they turned in for the night.

It wouldn't.

Chapter 20

That evening, as the sun was setting, a strong wind began to blow. It came out of the west, a front coming through with dark, ominous looking clouds. The wind blew open a few doors and scattered some trash but didn't much affect the deep snow that had become heavy with melt from the warmth of the day. Soon, to all of the former house pets' dismay, small flurries began to appear in the whistling night breeze. They all crossed their little paws, hoping beyond hope that this wouldn't be a repeat of the night before. What would they do if mother nature piled more snow onto what she'd already sent? There were many sinking feelings in empty little tummies.

Maybe their little pleas to the night sky were answered. Who knows how these things work, but the front blew quickly through, taking with it all the clouds and dreaded snow, leaving behind clear, star filled skies and a breathtaking quiet as the winds died out. This was followed by the cold.

Brrr, did it ever get cold. The pets hadn't experienced cold like this for weeks, and they didn't expect it. Ava, Sasha and Prince curled up together, working themselves under a thick comforter left on one of the beds in the house they now occupied. Shep and his little band of dogs moved all the beds into a far corner of the house, as far away from the open door as they could get, and snuggled up to each other for warmth. The gray kitty, all alone, had no one to snuggle up to, no one to comfort him. He sure missed the warm laps of his people this night, more than that he missed their companionship. He did what he could and dug deep into the towels and other linens in his closet and made himself reasonably comfortable. The pack of mean dogs didn't do much but suffer a sleepless night, growling at each other, hungry and cold.

The next day brought a bright morning sun, dazzling as it reflected off the pure white snow. The snow was now more like ice. After a filling breakfast, from the contents of the cupboard that was scattered about the kitchen, the dogs ventured outside. It looked like snow but Shep and his friends soon found they could walk on it without breaking through. The snow had become quite wet during the warmth of the day before and the night's cold had turned it to ice.

It was hard for the dogs to walk. It was ice, it was very slippery. Rat and Fluff, with their shorter legs, were much more adept at traversing the frozen groundscape. Soon they were running and chasing each other about. They found they could slide great distances, on their bellies, like penguins. All the dogs tried this, to varying degrees of success. Once again the dogs were having a great time, gales of barking laughter breaking the morning silence as they slipped and slid about.

A gray cat with bright green eyes, made even brighter by the sunshine glistening off of the icy snow, had heard the dogs and was cautiously approaching. He wanted to investigate what was causing all of the commotion. He snuck around the corner of a house, scampered behind some bushes, crawled under the deck of another house, hid behind some trees and eventually found himself in a spot with a view of the merry dogs slipping and sliding on the icy snow.

From his hiding place behind some small trees and bushes he watched as the dogs played, and in his own kitty cat way, he smiled. It was a beautiful day and after such a dreadful winter it was grand to see happiness return to the world. He thought for a moment about how amazed he was that the scary weather of the night before could turn so quickly into a day like this. He didn't know about geography, or great lakes, but, having lived in Michigan all his life, he was used to quick extreme changes in the weather. So, he was able to banish thoughts of cold and snow from his little head and enjoy watching the dogs play for some time. Being so near a tree gave him comfort. He could climb to safety in a hurry, but he didn't feel afraid, he was sure these happy dogs wouldn't hurt him.

The older dog called Slow came running in his direction, promptly slipped on the ice and went on a long slide followed by the little dogs Rat and Fluff. Slow came to a rest maybe 15 yards from where the gray cat hid and was pummeled by the sliding smaller dogs. They all laid there in a pile, laughing at themselves.

Slow was the dog that had been friendlest to the gray cat, he remembered this well. Maybe the little gestures that Slow had made wouldn't normally seem like much, certainly nothing that would bond two beings and make one want to warn the other of coming danger. To the gray cat, however, the kind way that Slow had treated him was all it took. The cat had been with a loving family, and had lost them. He had met nothing but hardship, hunger, cold, and other threatening animals since. Any showing of caring, of kindness, melted the gray kitties little heart. During a rare moment of silence the cat let out a small little meow.

The dogs all quickly looked in his direction and the gray cat was momentarily frightened, instinctively tightening his haunches, ready to spring from danger. This was short lived, Slow immediately recognized the cat, by sight and smell, smiled and greeted the cat as gently as he could. The gray cat relaxed.

Soon all the dogs came to greet the cat. They intermingled like old friends, the gray cat forgetting all about his natural mistrust of dogs.

After the greetings were all taken care of Shep asked the cat why he was there, what could have sent him from his comfortable home in such miserable conditions. The cat told the pack his story, about how the other dogs, which he'd told them all about before, had shown up. He told about the mean looking leader of the pack and his threatening comments towards this pack. He talked about his long journey, of how the snow had almost trapped him, and how he'd luckily found a house.

They invited the gray cat back to their house. He gladly accepted. What an odd looking pack they made as they slipped and stumbled their way across the icy snow back to the Den. Five dogs walking in a line, gingerly stepping on the slippery snow, the bigger dogs breaking through the upper crust on occasion as the warm sun had begun to soften the icy snow, and followed by a sure footed cat.

At the Den the dogs ate at their crackers and cereals and invited the gray cat to join them. He politely declined, having no interest in crackers and such, and asked if he could hunt in the house. He had already smelled and heard rodents scurrying about. The dogs all agreed to this and off he went.

Later, after a successful hunt, the cat rejoined the dogs in the living room. The dogs were mostly napping, the cat snuggled up to Slow and dozed.

When they woke they discussed the other pack more thoroughly. Shep had the cat retell the part about the pack leader talking about coming after them. They discussed this, wondering if they'd really make such a journey, but based on the cats description of the other pack's leader, his determination stood out. They expected the other pack would attempt to find them. This conclusion was very sobering to the dogs. They'd been enjoying themselves so much of late that they'd hardly given thought to the dangers of the new world they were in. TW hadn't shown up, there had been no sign of coyotes, and they hadn't met with any other dogs. Shep shrugged, this had been too good to be true, he should have know that they would be faced with mortal dangers sooner rather than later.

Once the reality of the situation had settled in they began to discuss what they should do. Sadly, very sadly, one by one the dogs realized that it would be unwise to stay here. The cat noticed this and mentioned how sorry he was to ruin the fun they'd been having. To this all the dogs thanked him again and again for the warning. It was beginning to sink in how much this cat had risked to help them. They gazed at him with wonder.

Shep told the cat that it was nonsense for him to feel sorry, the dogs would have been in very serious trouble if they would have been surprised by the other pack. Not that they weren't in trouble as it was, but at least they had a chance, a chance to work out a plan and take some action. The element of surprise had been removed, this was very important. Shep reassured the cat many times, thanked him many times, and told him they all owed him a big favor and would help him if he ever needed it.

After very little debate, as none of the dogs could think of what to do, they decided they would head back to the old den. This had been suggested by Goldie. There had been no sign of TW, surely he wouldn't be there all by himself, he would have either come to find them or have moved on. There was no way for the dogs to know about TW's change of heart and current fragile emotional state.

In a way, TW was slowly going crazy. Spending all of his time alone was hard enough, but the constant internal debate of whether to track down his old pack or leave them alone was an emotional rollercoaster. One minute elated that the other dogs might want to see him, the next minute devastated as memories of bad times flooded back. Times he'd mistreated the other dogs, physically and verbally abusing them, they'd never take him back. The memories would sink him into a deep depression, all thoughts of seeking out his former companions disappearing. Until the next day, and it would start all over again.

It was mid afternoon, the day was warming up nicely, maybe even above freezing. It didn't have to be that warm to melt the snow, the bright sun was doing a nice job of it. Anywhere there was something darker than pure white the snow was melting faster. At the base of trees, houses, and anything else that soaked up the sun's warmth the snow was quickly retreating. The dogs and their new friend ventured outside to enjoy the sunshine and the melting of the snow, which had been the enemy all winter long.

Shep let them know he thought it was too late to leave, they had a couple hours of daylight left but it would take a full day, if not longer, to reach the old den. They didn't want to travel at night. It was just as far to the gray cat's home, they decided to take their chances that the other pack wouldn't show up tonight. They must have been snowbound too, and wouldn't want to venture out so soon after the storm.

The other pack came to the same conclusion, all except their leader, he wanted to leave, travel all night if they had to. The pack was still hungry, they had caught a few rodents and, once the sun had warmed the icy snow, were able to dig up some buried crops, but it hadn't been near enough. They were tired too, and this combination made them very grouchy. When their leader pushed them they growled their disapproval, they all wanted to sleep the night away and maybe leave tomorrow.

The leader knew he could take any one of them in one on one combat, easily he thought, but not the entire pack, and pushing them this afternoon might possibly result in a mutiny. This is what he got for only allowing big, mean dogs in his pack. He wished for a moment that he wouldn't have chased off all the smaller dogs that wanted to join, they would have been much easier to bully. Once his anger subsided he realized leaving the next morning was probably a more reasonable course of action, it was going to be hard enough tracking this other pack and trying to do it at night might not be possible.

It had been a long time since he'd had to be reasonable. Running with this pack of dogs they had all nearly reverted to wild animals. They did as they pleased, hunted and scavenged and adventured at will. If one of the other dogs got out of line he quickly put them down. It was always only one though, if the entire pack turned on him it would be trouble.

They would busy themselves this late afternoon trying to fill empty bellies, sleep at this old farmhouse again tonight, then leave in the morning. He told the other dogs to be sure to pee all over everything in the house before they left, he wanted the cat, if he ever came back, to always know they'd been there. They all laughed at this.

As day once again faded to night all of the pets settled in. At the new den the gray cat was making himself at home. He shared Slow's bed, curling up behind Slow, near his shoulders. He heard a strange calming sound and realized he was purring, something he hadn't done since he'd lost his forever family. The dogs, all of which had already bedded down for the night, heard the sound too. Comforted and comfortable they stretched and yawned and were soon fast asleep, a peaceful little dog pack and their newest member, a purring gray kitty with bright green eyes.

The other pack wouldn't call it a day for some time yet. They were all still hungry and they hunted rodents and rooted around in the field till late in the night. Once they finally went inside no one would have said they were comforted and comfortable. They were tired and had only partially satisfied their hunger. The farmhouse was a mess, it smelled strongly of dog urine as a few of them had already been peeing inside, and they'd taken no time to put together any bedding. They found spots to lay, growling and nipping at their companions if they came too close, all the while being watched over by their impatient leader, which only added to the already palatable tension. If they didn't end up taking all of their aggression out on each other then beware to any other creatures they might encounter.

Prince, Sasha, and Ava were also out late. They hadn't left the house to go hunting the night before, the cold had kept them inside where they'd settled for a few very small rodents. They slept and napped and lounged about till nearly noon the next day, venturing out once it had warmed up outside. They hunted in a couple of nearby houses and were incredibly successful. The warm day brought out the rodents, they were very active.

As day became night and the darkness deepened the cats decided to sleep in one of the houses they were hunting. They didn't want to brave the tree and porch roof, which both had become quite treaturous with the snow turning to ice. Besides, with full bellies, they'd become sleepy, so they found a nice room with a comfortable bed and cuddled up together for the night.

The next day once again dawned bright with the rising sun. There had been cloud cover that night but it dwindled and disappeared with the morning sun. It was early but the pets could tell this would be the warmest day yet, just something they could feel in their bones. It was April now and old man winter was in retreat.

All of the pets rose this morning and greeted the day enthusiastically, happy to see the sun, and happy to be with their friends. Well, except maybe the wild pack of mean dogs, they rose aching and stiff from a night on cold, hard floors. They were all tired, having stayed up late and now being roused too early by their leader. They were also very hungry. Taking all of this together you could understand why they were all very cranky this morning, the nipping and growling even worse than the night before.

Their leader paid all of this no mind, and, after peeing generously on a sofa, led them outside. They headed off in the general direction they thought the other pack had gone, stopping quite frequently to root around in the fields for beans and corn and to sniff about for dog scent. Nothing was said, watching them no one would think they were friendly with each other, or anyone else. They ate, they nipped and growled at each other, they took care of their business, and made their way across one field then another.

This morning Shep and his friends finished off the feast on the kitchen floor while the gray cat finished off a few more rodents. Then they left the house, heading for the old den. They enjoyed each other's company much more then the wild pack and worked together to dig in the fields, feasting on beans they found and playing in the snow.

As the morning gave way to afternoon they were amazed at how quickly the snow was melting. The snow was getting mushy now. Here and there it had melted away leaving brown patches of exposed muddy field. Only a couple days ago there had been a foot of snow where these open patches of field were now. The early spring sun had launched a ruthless counter attack on the last winter offensive.

The dogs were trying to steer their path over snow covered areas, the muddy fields had become a quagmire which took too much effort to cross and at times had nearly swallowed up the smaller dogs. Fluff had become a brown muddy ball. She was miserable and soon took to rolling around in any somewhat clean snowy areas she could find, an attempt to clean herself off.

The gray cat had decided to come along. He'd been tempted to stay behind as he enjoyed the comfortable house with the large population of mice. In the end he decided to accompany the pack, not wanting to face the other pack alone. He stayed out of the fields, keeping to the fence lines and rows of trees. In the shadows the ground was much firmer and although he, on occasion, slipped on icy patches, it was preferable to being covered in mud, and he didn't need or want any old beans.

It was slow going, not sensing danger they took their time, eating and resting often. The wild pack was making much better time, the leader keeping them near fences and edges of trees in much the same way the gray cat was. The pack was getting hungrier and crankier but their leader kept them moving, coaxing them on with growls and nips, assuring them of feasts to come.

Meanwhile, the little cat pack of three had made it back to their new home. All the snow had melted off the porch roof and access was once again safe. With full bellies the cats quickly took to napping, as cats often will.

Chapter 21

Later that afternoon Sasha woke to bright sunlight streaming through the window over the porch. She attempted to cover her eyes with her little paws but it was no use, the light was too bright, so she decided to get up and look around. She walked over to the window and poked her little head through the small opening and sniffed at the spring air. Without people and all the people devices and machines the air smelled like Sasha thought it always should have, clean and refreshing.

She stepped out onto the porch to enjoy the last of the afternoon sun and feel the gentle breeze rustling her thick fur. She sat there on that porch roof for some time, very much enjoying a peaceful moment to herself. As the sun sank slowly in the western sky it began to get a little cooler out, but the roof shingles retained the sun's warmth keeping her little paws very comfortable.

There wasn't much to see, a few birds fluttering about, the dripping of water off the end of icicles, the patches of grass exposed by the melting snow, but this didn't matter. It was better this way, no trouble to be seen, just a time to relax and enjoy the day. After a time the other two cats joined her, saying nothing they sat and watched the sky turn a magical blend of many colors as the sun settled itself on the western horizon.

The coming of spring in such a cold climate lifted many spirits, none more than the former pets that had been forced to endure a winter without their warm homes and their humans. To the cats it was especially hard, losing their humans after having spent so much time training them was very difficult. They put negative thoughts aside and enjoyed the day. Rested and well fed, comfortable and safe on their perch, the cats had a most wonderful time doing mostly nothing at all.

As they sat a bird lit in the big tree near the porch and called out to them. It was Clarence. Sasha and Ava were overjoyed to see him, asking many questions in quick succession. How was he doing? Where had he been? When did he arrive? Clarence laughed and told them he was doing well but wanted to know about them and how they were doing before talking at length about his winter travels.

The cats said they were fine, winter had been difficult and they'd had their share of hardships, but they'd become very good hunters and had survived. Sasha saw Clarence's smile falter slightly at the mention of hunting. She smiled and quickly told him that they only hunted rodents, they'd never hunt their own friends. She said she'd starve to death first.

As they spoke Sasha noticed that Clarence seemed a little nervous, warily eyeing Prince. Sasha made introductions. She told Clarence about meeting Prince at the farm across the road and how the three of them had been together ever since. This had happened shortly after Clarence had said his goodbyes last fall and headed south for the winter.

Prince said he was very happy to meet him and mentioned how he'd loved the story that Sasha had told about Clarence the Robin. Prince had noticed that it was himself that was making Clarence nervous so he reassured the little birdy that any friend of these two was also a friend of his. His tone and his manner of speaking calmed Clarence and he soon fluttered over to a branch nearer the cats.

They talked a little more, but the sun was setting and Clarence said he needed to go off and find his mate and a place to roost for the night. They said their goodbyes, he promised to find them again the next day, then they'd share stories of winter adventures, and he flew off into the orange ball of the setting sun.

Sasha and Ava smiled as they watched him fly away. What a perfect ending to a perfect day. It would be hard to argue that animals didn't have emotions at a time like this. Sure they were more base, not as developed or complex as humans, but emotions nonetheless. Emotions were two trees growing in a vast wasteland. One of love, one of fear, and from their branches sprung leaves related. For the cats, on this day, spring had come to the tree of love and its branches had exploded with full green leaves.

If only the humans could experience emotions so simple and pure, but it was hard for them. For the humans the tree of fear grew fast and strong, branches sagging with the weight of a multitude of leaves, for fear manifests itself in many ways. Anger, hatred, unrest, anxiety, guilt, all grew from this tree. Complex were the humans' emotions and also their challenge. Enjoying the simple pleasure of the moment was almost impossible due to all the emotional clutter they carried with them each and every day. These emotions robbing them of the simple joy of living. The poor, complex humans lived a sadly ironic life, with nary a path for escape. Great intelligence that would seem to be the very thing that would help them rise above all of the leaves on the tree of fear, but ultimately it was that very intelligence that doomed them to constantly succumb to these joy robbing emotions.

Not the cats though, they were pure in their little minds and hearts, and this day and this time, was about joy. Nothing more, nothing less, simple and blissful joy.

As darkness spread the cats went out for an evening hunt, relaxed and refreshed. They were wary but encountered no troubles. The hunt went well and it wasn't long before they were back home. Tired and at peace they cuddled together on one of the big, people beds. It was earlier than usual but the cats were very tired and ready for sleep. Sleep came quickly for Prince. The other two tossed and turned for a while, anxious for the next day and the promise of long conversations and interesting stories shared with their robin friend.

As for the dogs the cats knew nothing about all the pack drama and couldn't care less. They hadn't even seen a dog since TW had left and had rarely wondered what the pack had been up to. The only time the dogs entered their minds was when they were leaving a house or other hiding place and were going out in the open, exposed and vulnerable. At these times they would look around and speculate as to where the pack had gone and although they had seen no sign of the dogs for some time, they were cautious, taught by the trials of many hard winter months, to always keep their guard up.

No, this was not a time of worry and fret, things that had often kept sleep at bay as they struggled through the long cold winter. This was a time of hope and wonder, as spring often is.

Shep and his friends didn't have as nice a day as the cats. It had started out okay as they set out for the old den. They had eaten well from the fields and played a little but after the smaller dogs had been bogged down in the mud the travelling had become more difficult. Fluff had removed much of the mud by rolling in the snow but as the day went on, the melting snow soaked the poor little girl's fur, chilling her to the bone.

Then there was the path the dogs had to choose. Trying to keep out of the mud as best they could, they were often following lines of trees and bushes which provided shade and kept the snow from turning to mud. Fluff would have preferred the warm sun to dry her fur. Her teeth began to chatter as the afternoon sun was dipping low in the western sky.

As the afternoon waned it became apparent they wouldn't make it to the old den until nighttime. Taking a break to discuss the dogs figured it would be late at night before they got there. This wasn't ideal as they didn't know what would be found once they arrived. They hoped the den would be deserted but Shep made them consider the possibility that it might be occupied by another pack, probably led by TW. They would have to approach warily. They considered stopping for the night but none of them wanted to sleep out in the open. If the den was occupied they'd just have to deal with it, turn back or head off in some other direction until a decent place to sleep was found. It was a sobering thought and the dogs' heads were hanging a little lower when Shep decided it was time to move on.

The dogs trudged on for what seemed like hours and their spirits were quite low. They were all cold and covered in mud, none worse than Fluff. She was putting on a brave face but the other dogs heard her chattering teeth and heavy breathing. It was hard for her to keep up. Slow trotted behind her and encouraged her best he could but there was no doubt that she was holding up the pack. The other dogs didn't mind, they were all fast friends now and mostly they just felt sorry for their little companion.

A short time later Shep stopped, his ears perking up a bit. He looked around a little and sniffed at the air. His intense concentration gave the other dogs pause and they began to look around with slight trepidation, fearful of what had caught their leader's attention. Then Shep told them he thought they were getting close, the landscape and scents seemed familiar.

Goldie muffled a short laugh of relief saying he thought Shep had seen a coyote or something worse. Shep laughed and apologized, then turned and trotted on towards home. The dogs all followed, feeling much better about their plight. Fluff's teeth even paused in their chattering. How quickly the sullen looks of despair had turned to smiles as they picked up the pace, hoping soon to find the old den, much the way they'd left it, just waiting for their return.

They became a little excited as they went. After many hours of relative silence the dogs were once again chatting amongst themselves, a mix of curiosity, excitement, and apprehension at what might be found once they made it to the old den. With so much on their little minds it's easy to understand why, when they heard the howl off in the distance, that it didn't immediately register as to what that meant. Their pace slowed, the chatting stopped and they looked this way and that, seeing nothing in the darkness. When they heard the next howl they stopped suddenly in their tracks, looking ahead into the darkness. At once the same thought crossed all of their minds, the den was occupied and they'd have to sleep in a cold field tonight.

The next howl was closer. The pack realized the howls were coming from behind them, it couldn't be from the old den. What was going on, the dogs were still confused and shocked. From despair to joyful excitement to dread and fear, the quick cycle of these emotions was making it hard for the dogs to focus and understand the current situation.

The gray cat, which most of the dogs had hardly remembered was even with them, got it first, he recognized the sounds. He screamed out that it's the other pack and starting sprinting ahead. The dogs were frozen in place for a moment but soon exploded forward as one, once their little brains had processed what the cat's scream had meant.

The dogs ran, they ran for their lives. Shep took up the rear, not willing to abandon Fluff. In her weakened state she couldn't keep up with the larger dogs. Goldie and Rat, whom were in the lead, slowed a little too. They all had silently decided to stay together and would face whatever was behind them as one, as a pack.

They ran on into the night, there was barking behind them now, the other dogs were getting closer. Run as far as they could, Shep thought, but it wouldn't do much good, the other pack was catching up quickly. Taking a quick look behind he caught the flash of wild looking eyes in the moonlight. When he looked forward again he saw, off in the distance, the shadows of houses, the houses of their old neighborhood. He smiled a slight sad smile, so close, but yet so far. They would have been home soon but they'd never make it now, the wild pack was close at hand. He began to steel himself for what was to come.

They ran up to a sparse row of small trees and bushes, beyond was a field of mud. Here, Shep decided, they had to make a stand, the other dogs were almost upon them and his smaller companions would never make it through the muddy field ahead. They crashed into the undergrowth and Shep turned on their pursuers, giving them the best of a vicious growl that he could muster.

The other dogs hardly paused, bounding out of the darkness they beset Shep and his friends. Two of them, in their haste, crashed into Shep, unable to stop as quickly as Shep had. Shep ripped at one of their flanks as they passed, scoring a hard bite. The bit dog howled loudly in pain and anger, then ran from the fray to lick his wounds.

Fluff and Rat both plowed into a small bush and were pursued by two dogs which couldn't get at the smaller dogs as bush was too thick. When one got his snout too close he nearly lost the end of his nose, Rat had struck like a cobra. That injured dog also ran off howling. The other, jumping and biting at the branches, was hardly a threat and seemed not to realize it.

The pack leader and one other dog had zeroed in on Shep. Goldie came to his aid. There was a standoff as they growled and barked at each other. The wild pack leader was circling in, getting closer. He would attack soon, Shep could sense it.

When the attack came it was sudden and furious, the two leaders engaged and fur began to fly. Shep was a thing to behold as he went at the other leader, his fury unleashed on his opponent in a wild blur of gnashing teeth. The other dog was surprised at Shep's counter attack. He'd expected a fight but one that would be quickly over. The pause was all Shep needed and he tore viciously at the other dog. The leaders broke apart and began another standoff. Goldie had held his own for a few moments with the other dog that had approached him and Shep but had been bitten hard on the leg and bolted for the bushes. He was pursued but his attacker turned and headed back to his leader once realizing he was in trouble.

While this was going on it looked like the end for Slow. A much larger and stronger dark black dog had backed him into a corner of trees and there was no escape. Slow growled but knew it was over, there was nowhere to run and this dog was so much bigger than him that there was little he could do. The dog was thick and strong looking, long fangs bared as he approached. He was going to tear him to pieces. Slow closed his eyes, he thought of his forever home, and his people, and all the love that he'd known and when the other dog lunged he was ready. It had been a good life.

The bushes to his left exploded and a bolt of TAN and WHITE collided with Slow's pursuer in mid air just inches from Slow's black and gray snout. The force of the blow sent the big black dog flying through the air, landing several feet away. It was like a car had hit that dog. For a moment Slow saw only the black fur and sharp white teeth of the big, terrifying dog lunging for him. Then an instant later, the horrible dog lay crumpled up in the mud, no longer a threat.

The other dog's last mistake in this world was to turn and attempt to fight back. It was TW, he was here, and without hesitation, and in a wild fury much more intense then what Shep had displayed, torn into the huge black dog, ripping its throat out and killing it in seconds. Besides their leader, this now dead dog had been their next best fighter, and, by far, the strongest amongst them.

TW turned, covered in fresh blood, a snarl on his lips that would loosen the bowels of any man, and looked at the remaining dogs in a way that left no doubt what was going to happen next. The other dogs had all stopped and were staring at TW, jaws agape. The saying 'a man amongst boys' was made for this moment. TW took one step towards his adversaries and they instantly scattered like the wind. There was no howling or barking, their wounds forgotten, the wild pack ran blindly into the night, trying desperately to outrun their fear for they had no other pursuer.

TW and his old friends stood in silence. Then TW closed his eyes and took a few deep shuddering breaths. He sat on the cold ground and bowed his big head and in a small voice said 'forgive me'.

The other dogs stared, not sure what to do. Fluff, Rat, and Goldie slowly crept from hiding places, warily watching the big dog that had once been the pack's leader. Shep stood where he was, waiting. Slow took a couple tentative steps towards TW, stopped, and told TW thanks, and that TW had saved his life.

TW slowly looked up and smiled and with tears streaming from his eyes, told Slow how happy he was to see him and began to profusely apologize for how he'd treated all the dogs, blubbering he said he was sorry again and again.

The other dogs looked at each other then back at TW. He was having some kind of breakdown, it appeared. He began to look small and vulnerable as he blubbered and apologized. Slow walked up to him and licked him and with encouraging and comforting words, as was his gift, calmed the big dog. Soon they rubbed muzzles together and TW leaned his head against Slow's shoulder and continued to sob. When he began to apologize again Slow cut him off and told him it's all okay, everything is going to be okay.

By now the other dogs had joined them and they were having a joyful reunion, something that none of them would have ever imagined could happen. This whole scene seemed surreal. Then Shep approached and caught TW's eye. TW quickly told him that this is your pack now, you'll always be the leader, I don't ever want to be that dog again, I just want to be with my friends. This all might have been hard for their people to understand but TW was now a protector, that was his role. Like a left tackle, with fangs, in the human game of football, he'd gladly sacrifice himself for his pack. And, also like a left tackle, the protector could be the most ruthless, vicious creature on the field, if his pack was threatened.

Oddly, in the silence that followed, there seemed to be no tension, just the pleading in TW's eyes met by the wonder in Shep's. When Shep said it's good to have you back with us all the dogs bounded up and began to prance about, sniffing and licking, tails wagging, hearts overflowing with joy.

Almost forgotten had been the gray cat who'd hid in a tree during all the commotion. He called down to Slow, quietly and timidly, unsure of how this latest development would affect him. Slow looked up and happily greeted the gray kitty, introducing him to TW. TW, to the surprise of all, bounded over like a big puppy, enthusiastically greeting the cat, telling him how happy he was to meet him. Slow told TW how the gray cat had warned them of the other pack's intentions, at great peril to himself. TW nearly started crying again when he told the cat how thankful he was for helping his friends.

Thus the gray cat relaxed and joined them, welcomed into the pack. They were complete, their troubles forgotten. Soon they headed off towards home, all the former pets happy and content, the other pack forgotten. The dead dog lay motionless, they paid it no mind, it would be left for the vultures.

The dogs carried on the joyful reunion well into the night. They made it back to the old den and it immediately began to feel like home again. Even the gray cat settled in quickly. Dawn was on the horizon before they had all dropped off to sleep. They'd sleep a good portion of the day away, exhausted from their incredible adventure.

Later, about mid morning, the cats began to stir. They were anxious to meet up with Clarence but decided to do their chores first. It wouldn't do to sit around waiting, hungry and unkempt. So they went out hunting. It was kind of a gloomy day, gray skies and a little cooler than the last couple of sunny days, but it was just fine for hunting. Hunting in the daytime was unusual for them but it seemed to make no difference. They tried a different, nearby house, and were quick to catch a meal. They were back home shortly after noon, relaxing, grooming, and thinking about an afternoon nap. The nap was quickly forgotten when they heard a familiar tweet.

The cats all climbed out the window onto the porch and found Clarence already waiting for them. He was examining the burgeoning buds on the tree branches and wondered aloud, as the cats were greeting him, when the buds would open and bring forth the green leaves of summer.

The odd little group talked for a long time that afternoon, telling stories and reminiscing about days gone by. At one point Clarence remarked at how fit the cats looked and how happy he was to find them doing so well. Secretly Clarence was amazed at this, he had expected to find them thin and ragged and weak, maybe not even alive, and here they were, looking more fit and stronger then when he'd left.

The cats had learned how to survive. Former pets would become wilder as time went by, living a hard life without people to care for them. Clarence speculated how long such a unique friendship would last before its bonds were pulled apart by the natural order of things. But for now he didn't care, he was enjoying the time with his friends, having conversations that surely, in this whole wide world, had never taken place before.

The cats all listened attentively as Clarence recounted his days down south. He explained that some birds, like himself, needed a warm place to winter as they molted, shedding feathers, and growing new ones in their place. One of the cats asked how he'd flown without feathers, Clarence only chuckled and said he couldn't.

It was a very dangerous time for a bird. It was hard to find food and avoid predators when one couldn't fly. He told about spending a lot of his time in a barn at a deserted farmhouse and how he'd had a close call with a c-c-creature he didn't recognize. (he'd almost said cat but decided at the last second to lie so as not to give his friends any cause for unrest). He was able to hop to a safe hiding place and the animal had moved on without ever discovering him.

Clarence mentioned seeing people on his journeys, this perked up the cats ears. He said they were few and far between. He'd seen a few very large compounds with many people and many more smaller groups widely scattered. He had no idea why they were grouped like this, he hadn't stopped near any of them to investigate. People had always frightened him.

He talked about growing in his new feathers and the relief he felt when he could finally fly again. It was such a wondrous freedom to be able to soar about the skies, he wished the cats could experience this. The cats, none of which were afraid of heights, said this wasn't something they desired. He figured this was just such an unnatural thought as to be outside of the cats' limited imaginations.

The cats told Clarence all about the troubles they'd had with the dogs and about how other birds and the squirrel had helped them once he'd flown south. They talked about what it had been like in the early days of winter, when it was bitter cold and their fur hadn't yet thickened. They had never been so cold.

The cats shared many memories, adventures at the farm, exploring different houses, run ins with other animals. Clarence was especially interested in hearing about the showdown at the farm. The dogs had come looking for the cats and the coyotes had run them off. He commented that it all sounded very fascinating but must have been terribly scary.

The cats talked at length about the odd behavior of the big tan and white dog they called TW. He was the reason they'd ended up here. The dog had come back to the farm by himself and was pretty obviously not going to leave as long as the cats stayed. They had decided to leave, then found this house with only the one entrance way up high, out of a dog's reach, and so had made it their new home.

The big dog had come looking for them. He'd tracked them to the tree out front. He'd stood vigil for some time but then the oddest thing had happened. The dog had a breakdown of some sort, or maybe a change of heart, had bid them farewell and left. Clarence mentioned that this all sounded rather fishy and wondered if it was some kind of trick. To which Sasha replied, as she had with the other cats, that she was sure it was not. Something about the way the dog had spoken, well, it was hard to explain. It was just something she knew. Clarence said he'd keep and eye out for anything suspicious.

The friends talked and talked until they ran out of things to say, all of them thinking how good it was to have friends. After a time Clarence said he had to go, they were going to pick out a spot to build a nest. He apologized, he'd be very busy in the weeks ahead, preparing a nest and hopefully having a family, but he'd stop in to say hello when he could. The cats smiled sad little smiles, they knew the truth of this. Life often raises obstacles to friendship, but they would do their best to maintain the relationship. Regardless of what happened, Sasha and Clarence would have a lifelong bond, developed between a baby bird and a cat shut out from her home, a lifetime ago, on a warm early summer night.

Chapter 22

For the next few weeks life went along pretty smoothly for both the dog and cat packs. The dogs adjusted quickly to their new pack order and TW was the main reason. He seemed happy all the time, simply excited to be with his friends. The only difficulty was that food was becoming more of a challenge.

Spring had sprung, the snow had melted away, plants were popping up out of the muddy ground and leaves were beginning to fill the barren branches of trees. One problem with this warmer weather was that the field beans and corn that they had relied upon through most of the winter months were beginning to rot. Beans in the mud were lost, only standing plants were salvageable. The corn was their best bet but even the ears on standing plants had begun to mold. This prompted the dogs to expand their range and begin hunting more. The deer population was very large, they had survived the winter well, mainly due to the field grains left behind by the departing people. There had not been a harvest last fall so there was plenty left, but more significantly for the deer, neither was there a fall deer harvest as the hunters were also gone.

Shep was a creative and intelligent hunter and with the assistance of TW's brawn, they had taken a few deer. Mostly culling the older or the lame, deer that probably would not have survived this last winter if there would have been farmers around to harvest the crops. The dogs also scavenged a few dead deer they came across, killed by coyotes and only partially consumed.

The dogs were careful with the coyotes, trying to stay away from them as best they could, but did not let the coyotes stop them from their own hunting. Previous confrontations with wild animals had taught them that they could handle themselves in that situation, but there was no need to take unnecessary risks, so they avoided coyotes if they could.

Actually, they felt more confident now than when they had battled the coyotes in the winter. The coyote scents they detected on their travels showed them that the coyotes were mostly hunting in pairs with the occasional pack of three. With Shep and TW the dogs felt sure they could deal with a pair, and even three if they had to.

TW had taken on a different air since rejoining the pack, he was now the pack's protector. If any danger presented itself he was first to confront.

One evening the pack stayed out a little later than normal, heading back to the Den only after darkness had fallen. On the way back they had met a single coyote. Goldie and Slow had been up front and were engaged in a snarling, growling standoff. The coyote had even taken a step forward as if he were about to attack. TW had been bringing up the rear, guarding and helping the smaller dogs along. He heard the noise and stepped up between Slow and Goldie. He eyed the coyote, gave that familiar chilling snarl, and began to walk forward with a fearless determination that instantly told the coyote he'd better run if he wanted to save his ass.

Shep, stepping up in time to witness this, saw the coyote go from hunter to hunted in a split second, his attitude changing instantly from carnivore to scared little rabbit. The coyote turned and bolted, actually peeling out on the muddy path, sending clumps of dirt flying as he tried desperately to gain traction. TW did not pursue. The coyote turned his head as he picked up speed and gave a slight yelp as if TW were hot on his heels. It had been the look he saw in TW's eyes, he knew that dog would not just hurt him, he'd kill him and that was that. From then on word spread amongst the coyotes, beware the big tan and white dog with the crazy eyes.

To the pack those eyes were anything but crazy. To each of the dogs those eyes said I'll give my life for you.

Some of the coyotes, attempting to avoid the crazy eyed dog, had wandered near the cats' neighborhood. Here they found rodents a plenty, virtually streaming from the vacant house in search of food in the nearby fields. It took quite a few to make a decent meal but there were so many that it didn't take long.

One night, the cats, after leaving one of the vacant houses they liked to hunt, saw two sets of yellowish green eyes peering at them from a nearby field. They were a fair ways off but that was of little comfort. They all wanted to go home but weren't sure if they dared. They didn't want to go back inside the house they'd just left, access would be easy for the coyotes. Quickly they talked it over.

The coyotes hadn't moved. Prince told them that if the coyotes came after them they had no choice but to dart back inside and hide best they could, preferably up high. There were some cabinets inside that would do. He suggested they sneak along the edge of the house and once they got to the corner, if the coyotes still hadn't come for them, then make a break for it. They weren't far from home and they should be able to easily beat the coyotes to the big tree and safe house. If the coyotes came after them before they got to the corner then they should turn around and head back inside this house. The cats all agreed and slunk along the edge of the house.

At the corner the coyotes still hadn't moved so they made their break. Running as fast as they could they dashed across open territory, fearing that at any second they'd hear the footfalls of a fast approaching enemy swiftly gaining. They made it to the front yard with the big tree and Prince looked back, the coyotes hadn't even bothered to move but were still watching intently. He told the others and they all chuckled slightly at the overreaction but nonetheless scurried up the big tree into the nice safe house without hesitation. It had been a while since they'd received a fright like that.

Once back inside, and after their breathing had returned to normal, the cats spoke about this recent development. They all agreed that they would have to be more careful from now on. Ava suggested that maybe they should hunt during the day as the coyotes had only been seen at night. This seemed reasonable to the other two.

They also decided to stick to hunting in houses. It was becoming harder to hunt mice in the houses but they had to consider their safety first. With the warming weather and dwindling inside food supplies, more and more rodents were leaving for the fields, making the houses less attractive hunting grounds.

With decisions made they curled up to sleep the rest of the night away and maybe a good part of the next day too, as cats often liked to do. They didn't sleep as much as they used to, back in the days when people would keep food bowls full and hunting was mostly something done in their dreams. It was okay though, they didn't mind replacing a little sleep with some adventure. Although they probably would not have said the same thing a few short months ago, when it was bitter cold and tummies were rarely full, and they seemed to have some animal or another always hunting them.

During the night, only one cat woke. Ava jumped up with a start, a coyote nipping at her tail as she ran. It took her a moment to realize it was only a dream as she heard Sasha mew in her sleep at the disturbance. She soon curled up in a tight little ball and fell back to sleep. This time she dreamed of sleeping in a lap with one of her people gently scratching behind her ears. This was a much better dream, and she did not wake.

The next morning Sasha and Prince woke to Ava scratching. The warmer weather had brought back her old scourge, the flea. The other two were also becoming annoyed with the pests but weren't bothered near as much as Ava who dug and dug at them until patches of fur were missing. In the days that followed she begun to draw blood as she dug at some of the bare patches.

On one of Clarence's visits he noticed Ava's problem and suggested they try the creek trick. Clarence hadn't witnessed this and was hoping the cats would give it a try, he really wanted to watch. Prince said they had thought about it but with the coyotes, which they'd seen a few more times, nearby they weren't sure they wanted to go that far from the nice safe house. Clarence said he could be their eyes in the sky. He couldn't be gone long as him and his mate had four beautiful little sky blue eggs in their nest and he had to help take care of them. He mentioned that there was also a larger egg, white with brown spots, in the nest. It made him uneasy but his mate insisted it was theirs and would be treated equally.

Upon hearing this a little bell went off in Sasha's head. She often like to curl up with her people while they watched TV. Nature shows were on quite a bit and she enjoyed these. One of these shows talked about the cowbird, a bird that would lay an egg in a host nest and have the host parents raise the baby like one of their own.

This sounded rather distasteful to Sasha, and it only got worse. The cowbird would often hatch first and quickly outgrow the host birds own chicks. It would aggressively steal all the food the parents brought back to the nest for itself, sometimes even knocking the smaller birds from the nest, killing them. In the end the host parents would often end up raising only the cowbird chick.

Sasha, out of deep concern for her friend, earnestly relayed this story to Clarence. Clarence's beak opened and he blinked his eyes in horror as the story unfolded. He trusted Sasha and said he'd go back to his nest and knock that egg out. He would tell his mate this story and if she didn't agree then he'd knock it out when it was his turn to sit with the eggs and deal with her wrath when she got back. So off he went, a bird on a mission.

A few days later the cats decided to scout the area and see if there were any dangers on the way to the creek. Ava was getting worse and something had to be done. They set out one cloudy gray morning. Rain threatened but the clouds held their payload and only grew darker.

The route they took would take them past their forever home, a place they hadn't been near in months, as they'd mostly stayed within a few houses of the safe house. Sasha and Ava were excited by this prospect and wondered what they would find. Maybe their people had come home. Prince, also excited that he might catch a glimpse of his old farm, tried to let them down easy. He told them not to get their hopes up as they'd seen no sign of humans. Oddly, just a few minutes later, the cats heard a distant rumbling noise. The noise, growing slowly louder, inspired fear and caused them to hid in some nearby bushes.

Eventually the sound came and went. At its apex the sound was coming from the direction of the main road. It then quickly diminished as it headed in the other direction. The cats hadn't been near this road since the last time they'd crossed it when leaving the farm. They poked their heads out, looked around and then at each other. It had taken them a minute but eventually the cats realized what that sound was, a vehicle. They stayed hidden for a bit longer, listening intently for more people sounds, but there were none. What did it mean? None of them could understand why the people would be gone so long then just one lonely vehicle go rumbling through?

When Ava began to scratch again they decided to press on. Soon they made it to their old home. The cats went inside and were saddened by its state. It smelled strongly of rodent and other animals. The skunk smell was strong, Prince figured one or more had wintered here. From the other animals the cats had met they all understood the concept of hibernating. Sasha and Ava looked worried at this and quietly wondered if they were going to surprise and wake some hibernating animal. Prince chuckled and said that any animal that had spent the winter here was long gone, woken by the first warm day, sent out into the world to scavenge for food by an empty belly. Privately he wasn't sure about this, he'd only wanted to reassure the other cats.

They poked around for a few minutes, Sasha and Ava reminiscing as they went. Here was the big chair they loved to lounge on and watch the birds eating at the feeders. Now it was covered in a thick layer of dust and smelled strongly of rodent urine and mold.

Here was the sun room where they'd spent long summer afternoons napping and watching cars zoom by on the busy road. The room was in shambles, a branch from the big maple that overhung the porch having taken out two of the windows. There was a thick layer of leaves on the floor and everything seemed wet and moldy. Prince hopped up on a table and looked out one of the intact windows. From here he could see the farm. He sat for a minute and silently reminisced.

Soon they all decided they would head back. There was still hours of daylight left but the nostalgia of this visit and the sadness it had brought on took the wind out of their adventure sails. Besides, they hadn't enlisted Clarence's help for today, telling him it would only be a short scouting trip. The creek wasn't far from here and no danger had presented itself so they would go back home and plan with Clarence for maybe tomorrow or the next day.

When they left the old forever home they stopped across the road at the first house they'd entered after the people had left. This was the house with the big branch across the window sill. They followed the branch and went inside. They had also met the possum here, although they did not expect to see him as the hibernating animals had moved on. They were pleasantly surprised when he called out to them from a dark corner.

They spoke for a while, catching up on each other's comings and goings. The cats quickly introduced Prince and warned about the coyotes. The possum knew about them, he explained that he'd been out and about for some time now but often returned to this house as here he felt safe. The cats could understand that.

The possum mentioned the noise on the road, he'd heard it not only today but the night before. This surprised the cats, they'd only heard today's sounds. What could it mean? They were hopeful that their people would return but didn't mention this to the possum as they knew he dreaded the return of people.

After a time the cats all said their goodbyes and left the possum with wishes of good luck and good will. He told them to stop in again as he always enjoyed their visits.

On the way back home the cats talked over some plans. Set up a day with the birds. Leave early in the morning. Go quickly, no stops to investigate or reminisce. No time wasted, get back home early. This would be a time in which the night predators, tired from nighttime hunts, would be sleeping soundly wherever they called home and least likely to be out and about hunting cats.

Walking around the corner of a house, heading towards the small, side road that would lead them home, all three cats froze in their tracks. There, in the middle of the road stood TW, a very imposing figure. TW spotted the cats immediately and let out a happy bark of greeting, wagging his tail profusely. This confused the cats greatly, except for Sasha. This is exactly what she'd tried to convey to the other two, this dog had undergone some remarkable change.

Still suspicious the former pets spoke as animals do, with looks, body language, and senses people would never understand. TW told them he was very happy to see them and that they were looking well. He rambled on for a bit, talking about his pack and how happy he was to be with them and how they'd never hurt the cats. They'd even adopted a cat of their own, a great gray kitty with bright green eyes. Finally he stopped chatting and asked the cats if they'd heard the noise, that's why he was here with his pack, to investigate. They had been out exploring and were in this general area so they'd ran towards the sound to check it out. At this moment the rest of the pack joined him in the street, Shep in the front. Slow soon saw the cats and greeted them enthusiastically, tail wagging fast.

Although neither group approached the other the meeting was amicable enough. The dogs could sense the nervousness of the cats and instinctively gave them some space. Comings and goings were discussed, even the subject of weather was brought up. The main topic was the noise on the road. The dogs hadn't seen the vehicle either but they were all excited about what it might mean. Would more soon follow? Were the people finally coming home?

Eventually the conversation worked its way around to coyotes, the most pressing concern of the cats. Rat, for the first time, joined in on the discussion, bragging up TW profusely as he relayed the story of the last coyote the pack had encountered and how it had turned tail and ran when TW confronted it. He embellished somewhat but the cats, for the most part, believed the story. TW, although having such a profound change to his personality, looked even more intimidating now than when the cats had first met him, if that was possible.

Rat was the most excited of the dogs to have TW back, he and TW had bonded as friends since his return. Not like the leader slash sycophant roles they had before. They ran together and even played, on occasion. It was heartwarming to watch. They accepted their roles in the group without hesitation, Shep was the leader and there was no conflict.

TW and Rat were valuable members of the pack. TW was the main force when it came to dealing with larger animals but Rat had found his niche in rooting out smaller animals from hiding places, often funneling them right to a waiting TW.

Slow and Shep had come together to form a practical alliance. Shep had come to rely on the older dog's wisdom and valued his opinion. They'd also become closer friends, frequently engaging in conversations one would have thought more appropriate for people. Goldie would often join them for these chats.

Lately Goldie had formed an unlikely bond with Fluff, quickly becoming fast friends. They liked to look out the windows at night, watching the sunset and, if they weren't too tired, gazing at the moon. During these times they liked to reminisce about the missing people. The other dogs would overhear them and feel waves of nostalgia. If it weren't for these conversations the dogs would have nearly forgotten about their people, it had been so long and they'd been through so many adventures.

Goldie and Fluff, copying Rat and TW, formed a small animal hunting team too. Not as proficient as the other two they still enjoyed occasional success and it made them feel useful to the group. This was something all the dogs wanted to feel, and the more the better. Once in a while they would also run and play with Rat and TW as Shep and Slow would look on smiling.

After a good long time and many discussions, the cat pack and dog pack parted company on very good terms. As they turned to leave, the dogs let the cats know that they'd pass through here again and try and give the coyotes a good scare. The cats were very appreciative of this gesture.

One the way home the cats stopped at a house just down the street from their safe house, one they hadn't hunted before. This proved to be a good decision as the house was teeming with rodents. The hunt was quick and successful and there were still a couple of hours of daylight left when they made it home.

As they were watching the sunset from the porch roof, what they could see of it through the cloud cover anyway, Clarence came to visit. He asked how the scouting trip had went and was surprised to hear how far the cats had gone. He pleaded with them not to go again without letting him know, he worried for his friends in this brave new world.

The cats assured him that he'd know, and they all decided, weather permitting, that tomorrow would be the day. The cats bid Clarence good night and he fluttered away. Full tummies and big adventures combined to allow tired kitties to turn in early for the night.

A good night's sleep and the cats were up early the next day, eager for another even bigger adventure. Clarence hadn't showed up yet so they went to hunt the house from the day before. Again it didn't take long and they were full, ready to meet the day.

They were going to go back home and wait for Clearance but he met them in the front yard of the house they had just hunted. He gave them a concerned look and they quickly explained that they had just come here for breakfast and weren't planning on leaving without him. The cats were all warmed and smiled slightly, sensing the worry in Clarence's voice.

After this quick conversation the cats and their eyes in the sky started towards the creek. Clarence gave them a code, one tweet for all clear, two for trouble. He flew up and away, going ahead a little, then side to side. Once in a while he'd call out with one loud clear tweet to reassure his friends.

The cats marvelled at how far Clarence could travel. The trip to their old house had taken them an hour, he could make it in a minute or two. Maybe flying was a good thing. Of course, yesterday when they'd gone on their little adventure, they had been sneaking along from house to house, tree to tree, bush to bush, often stopping and surveying their surroundings, looking for danger. This took some time. With Clarence they went much faster, confidently trotting along the sidewalk. Not quite without a care in the world, as the saying goes, they still constantly looked this way and that, always wary, but moved much quicker then they'd have ever dared without Clarence. It took maybe a little more then a quarter hour to make it to their old home. Here the cats took a moment to rest and survey the area, looking about for danger. They had been fascinated at how quickly the journey had gone and having plenty of time, felt no particularly need to foolishly rush into any possible danger.

Having not realized how fast they could move, with the help of their bird friend, the cats figured, if all went well, they'd be home by noon, just in time to take a well deserved afternoon nap. Clarence told them to wait here and he'd fly ahead to the creek and have a look around the nearby area. Off he went, the cats making themselves comfortable on the front porch of their old home. Today they had no desire to go inside, the house was in shambles and seeing it only served to destroy fond memories of having a forever home. These they wished to preserve, having good memories to recall often helped one make it through difficult times.

Soon Clarence came back and gave the all clear. The cats set off for the creek. They crossed through the large bordering yard, crept under a broken old fence, then around a shallow pond, stopping for a minute to talk with their fish friend. Soon after they were at the bank of the creek.

The brush was thicker than they'd remembered, and the water looked a little deeper and swifter, but otherwise it was much the same as the last time they'd rid themselves of the nasty biting little fleas. They found a spot just after a bend in the creek. Here on their side of the creek, was a small pool that looked deep enough to work. The swifter water routed towards the opposite bank by a bend in the creek. This helped keep the little pool undisturbed.

The cats first all found twigs that would serve as little flea boats. Prince was eager to try. Like most cats he didn't much care for water but the story the other cats had told had been fascinating and he'd hoped he would have a chance to try it one day. Ava, however, would be first, Sasha telling Prince that she did this perfectly last time and that he should see at least one of them show him how it was done. This flattered Ava and she puffed out her little chest with pride.

They all agreed that Ava would go first and, with twig in mouth, she approached the water. With one loud tweet, signaling the all clear, Clarence swooped down to watch the show. He had other birds enlisted to help with the watch, they would take turns.

As she had last fall, with infinite patients, Ava waded slowly into the water, grimacing at the cold. The nasty little bugs scurried up her legs to avoid the water. Then up her sides to her back. Finally only her head was above the surface of the cold little pool. She approached the edge of the pool pointing her little nose towards the swifter currents. Slowly she went under the water until only the tip of her snout and the twig were exposed. She watched as the last of the fleas jumped onto the twig. She then released the twig into the swifter currents on the far edge of the pool and, with eyes open under the water, watched as her nemesis quickly floated away. She turned and exited the water as quickly as she could.

Sasha and Prince repeated the process. Prince, surprisingly, had been a big baby about entering the water, and it took some extra time for him to finish up. Much to his chagrin he had been jeered by watching birds of many different feathers as he timidly worked his way into the water. Heckled by birds, that was a real blow to his ego. He smiled warmly as he thought this.

As Prince was finishing, eager to get a good look at the twig full of fleas as it floated off, he got too close to the swifter currents at the edge of the pool. One misstep, a paw slipping off a slimy rock, and he fell forward right into the strength of the current. He was immediately swept away, head bobbing in the water, he frantically paddled for shore. As the creek wasn't all that big he soon regained his footing and stumbled towards the bank. Only once he set foot on dry land did he finally hear the gales of laughter, bird and cat alike, directed at him. He shook off the water and dug a little at one of his ears but soon sat up and smiled at the others, aware of and humbled by his exploits.

Neither Sasha or Prince had nearly as many fleas as Ava but they were both, nonetheless, very grateful to be rid of them. The fleas would return, of course, there was no avoiding it. For now the cats would enjoy a respite and return when they had to.

They relaxed on the bank, grooming and speaking with Clarence about the days events. This, Clarence had said, was about the most interesting thing he'd ever witnessed. Just then a bright red cardinal swooped down, tweeting loudly, twice!

Coyotes he called. The cats tumbled all over themselves in their haste to run up the creek bank. The Cardinal called to them, he wanted them to go a different way, and to calm down, the predators weren't close. He apologized for scaring them half to death but he'd been out of breath from flying fast and trying to tweet at the same time. He'd made a large arc to the south of where the cats were as none of the birds had seen any movement nearby. That's when he saw something brown near the woods' edge further south, just past the old farmhouse. Prince's ears perked up, this was his old home.

There had been three coyotes prowling there, oddly in the middle of the day. Their path would lead them past the farm and near to Sasha and Ava's old forever home. The cats needed to decide on a different route back to their current home with the big tree out front, and they needed to do it quickly. They turned and headed along the creek bank to the north. They would follow the creek this way until they came to a little bridge over a smaller side road. From here they could skirt quickly up the bank, cross the road, and make a dash for their house. It wouldn't be far.

A couple birds scouted the path ahead and there were no further incidents as the cats made there way along the creek bank. At the little road, after some further reassurance from Clarence, they took off at a run for home. They were breathing very hard as they scrambled up the tree and onto the porch roof. They turned and paused for a minute, looking out in the general direction of their old forever home. Soon enough three coyotes came trotting out from in between two houses. The cats crouched low and the coyotes, apparently not noticing them, trotted along the street then back through the houses maybe a hundred yards away.

This was not good, not good at all. Coyotes patrolling in their very own neighborhood, a bad sign it was. They were safe in this house. There were no broken windows or open doors that the coyotes could reach, for now. However, they had to eat, and there wasn't much left to hunt in this house. They would have to venture out when they could. Clarence said he had to go home, he'd been gone far too long, but he'd come back before the day was over and, once again, be their eyes in the sky.

He fluttered away and the cats discussed amongst themselves. They couldn't rely totally on Clarence, this was a very busy time for him. They would have to work out a plan. For now it looked like neither night nor day was safe, coyotes could be out at anytime. They would have to tread very carefully and do their best not to be caught out in the open. All of this would have to wait, they were very tired from the day's' adventures and cats, being cats, needed a cat nap before anything else could be decided. So off they went to curl up together and sleep the afternoon away, as cats often do.

Chapter 23

For the next few days the cat and dog packs went about their business mostly untroubled. Both packs heard, on more than one occasion, the distant rumblings of vehicles, but none had yet caught a glimpse of people. Whatever they were doing it was only a trickle of activity and it seemed unlikely they'd return enmasse, refilling their vacant houses.

They all heard the coyotes howling at night. They were mainly a problem for the cats. The dogs had faced them down and were wary but generally unconcerned. The dog pack had visited the cats a couple more times but had not run into any coyotes. It was generally assumed the coyotes were avoiding the dog pack but they were still lurking around, coming out after the dogs had left.

For the cats, hunting had become a daytime activity. The coyotes seemed much less active when the sun was up. One fine morning they exited a house they'd just finished hunting to a beautifully brilliant sun. They sat, huddled up in the doorway, as their eyes adjusted quickly to the bright light. The hunt had been decent but it was getting harder to find a meal inside. They yearned to hunt the fields but with the coyote threat this wasn't a good idea.

Prince saw it first, the other two soon after. Not fifty yards away a coyote was standing quite still, in the shade between a small tree and some bushes, at the edge of what was once a well manicured lawn, but was now more of a field. Staring and panting, he watched the cats. He took a small step forward, the cats moved backwards, into the shadows beyond the doorway. The coyote came no further. It watched the door for a few minutes, a time that seemed much longer to the cats, then turned and loped away.

This wasn't the only recent coyote encounter, but it was the closest. The cats had found that there was no need to try and make a break for home, any house would do. For coyotes, people had not yet been gone long enough for them to approach and enter any house, fear of people too firmly implanted in their little minds.

The cats had discussed this at length and felt reasonably assured that they were safe inside, but this wouldn't last forever, they knew that. They would have to observe the coyotes closely, watch them to see if they were getting over their fear. This confrontation seemed to affirm their suspicions. It wouldn't be long until the coyotes were approaching open doorways. How long would it be until one of them stepped over a threshold and opened up a new world for all of them?

With this in mind the cats always made a point of looking for high up hiding places and alternate escape routes in all the houses they entered. When house hunting became unsafe they would be in serious trouble.

It wasn't that long ago that they worried that soon they would have to hunt outside, exposing themselves to the threat of carnivores. For the most part the indoor food supply for the rodents had completely dried up, yet they were still able to hunt inside somewhat successfully. They had to work at it harder and it was taking much more time but they continued to be decently fed and only occasionally went hungry. The prevailing theory was that the rodents liked living inside. Mice would glean the fields and nab insects then return to the houses they had adopted, enjoying the fruits of their labors.

This was one reason the houses they entered were getting more and more disgusting. Damp floors, basements with standing water, the smell of mold and rodent urine, all combined to make a very unpleasant atmosphere. The former homes were also, as they became more open to the elements, getting a thick layer of dust, dirt, and other debris.

The repeat of freezing at night, thaw during the days, of early spring had been hard on doors and windows. Cracks in glass spread, grew larger by the day, then a chunk would fall out, letting in the wind and rain. Door frames full of moisture, frozen solid at night, then quickly warmed by the morning sun would shift and splinter and doors would soon be slightly ajar. Winds would take them, pulling or pushing, until they were wide open. In would come the rain and whatever the wind would blow, dirt and leaves mostly. Some had gathered so much debris and dirt that small plants had already begun to take root under dining room tables and on kitchen floors. Houses that were, such a short time ago, full of the sounds of humans and their families, playing children and the grumbles of adults figuring out how to pay bills, were quickly becoming just another small ecosystem of mother nature.

Other mammals, raccoons, possums, squirrels, were beginning to frequent houses, using them like the rodents were, a place to crash once their bellies were full. Also a place to hide from predators. These creatures seemed to have gotten over the fear of humans much quicker than the larger coyotes.

The bloom of spring life was everywhere, quickly taking over the habitats that people, and, of course, their pets, had once held domain. At first this was great for the cats, the exploding rodent population kept them fed, but as time went by problems began to surface. More rodents drew in more predators. Taller plants gave the cats more cover, but also hid their enemies. Even creatures that weren't hunting the cats became a danger.

One day Ava disturbed a slumbering raccoon which was napping peacefully on a large chair in someone's old living room. The raccoon had jumped up suddenly, sending Ava dashing for cover. Being just as startled as the cat, the raccoon took off for the nearest door, a path that led right at poor Sasha. She was none too quick in processing the situation, springing about five feet straight up in the air a split second before the raccoon bowled her over. She'd landed in almost the exact spot she'd lept from, and, having done a 180 in the air, watched the raccoon's rear end disappear out the doorway just as her feet made contact with the soggy carpet floor.

The cats were all very thankful that their adopted home had stayed relatively intact. The doors were still firmly shut and none of the windows had been broken. The open window above the porch remained the only entry point. One the cats, as far as they knew, were the only animals to discover.

One fine spring day they decided to venture a little further from home than normal. They set out mid-morning, heading in the opposite direction of their old forever home. They bypassed several houses that they knew well, having previously hunted them many times, in search of more fertile hunting grounds. It was slow going as they warily moved from house to house, often stopping to look for signs of trouble.

The cats followed a long looping road that went through the heart of the subdivision and soon came to a small bridge over the familiar creek. This road would eventually loop around to an area on the other side of the creek from their old forever home. If they wanted to, they could stop in for a visit, but they'd have to get wet crossing the creek, a condition that generally does not appeal to cats.

They would have to cross the bridge to get to houses they hadn't hunted before. Hiding in some bushes they surveyed the area for some time before deciding to move on. Quickly, they scurried across the bridge. The cats hated being out in the open like this, so exposed. At a full run they headed for the first house they came to, hurried up the steps and hid, acting much as if they were actively being chased. Peering out from around corners and under old forgotten furniture they soon discovered there was no immediate danger.

The cats came out from their hiding spots and then spent some time lounging on the porch. The sun was bright this morning and the day was already warming up nicely. The cats were shedding their thick winter coats, fur coming out in great clumps, but they still had plenty of fur to keep them warm. A little too warm on a sunny day like this. Ava had been panting as the cats hid but had gathered herself after the short break and was anxious to hunt.

The cats walked slowly around the house and luckily found a ground level window open. A entire section of the window had fallen to the ground. Its frame had loosened so that the window appeared to have slid down over time and eventually toppled out of the frame into the raggedy looking bushes. The cats jumped through into the dark house.

Familiar smells greeted them. Dampness and mold, rodent stink, the faint scent of a few larger animals that had probably, hopefully, moved on. The cats cautiously explored. They soon heard the scurrying of small prey but that was the only sound, other than the occasional drip drip of water.

Feeling safe they went in separate directions and began to hunt. The rodent population was good, not bursting at the seams like some houses they had hunted in the dead of winter, but better than what they were currently used to. Also, they had caught the mice unawares. They weren't as cautious as the rodents had become in houses that were hunted regularly. These mice had been free of predators, it had made them easy targets, and the cats soon enjoyed another successful hunt.

They left the house and gathered on the front porch to discuss the hunt. Recounting the adventures they had was one of the cats' favorite pastimes. Ava, especially, loved telling the other two how she had cornered this mouse or jumped up to snag that mouse, it never got old. She was still flush with excitement when they went on a hunt, much more so than the other two cats. Having been an indoor kitty and, for such a long time, wanting to get outside and hunt, the newness of adventure had not yet left her. Yes, there was a time during the middle of winter, not wanting to venture out into the cold night to hunt, that she'd have greatly enjoyed a warm bowl of food placed in front of her by her loving humans. But the weather was now much better and she was always ready to get her hunt on.

The cats decided it was time to head back, they got up and started down the front steps, Prince in the lead. He stopped so suddenly that Ava's head butted him in the backside. There, up ahead in the middle of the bridge, stood a coyote, eyeing them. The cats, frozen in place, returned the stare. When the coyote took a step towards them they all sprang to action. Darting off the porch Prince led the way to the back of the house. Sasha, daring a look behind, saw that the coyote had broke into a run and was in hot pursuit.

The cats, not having far to go, quickly made it to the open window and jumped through. Prince jumped up on some shelving which he hoped would be high enough to avoid the coyote. Ava and Sasha took off up the stairs to find other hiding places.

Prince, looking out the open window, soon saw the coyote come into view. It had ran quickly into the back yard and stopped maybe ten yards from the open window, peering into the blackness within. As Prince watched, the coyote took a few tentative steps forward, sniffing the air, its head bobbing up and down and side to side. It stopped well short of the window, and, after a few more sniffs and looks, turned and trotted back in the direction from which it had come.

Prince waited a few minutes, and, after feeling the threat had passed, jumped down and went upstairs to find the other two. He found them huddled together way up high on top of some kitchen cabinets. Scared, the cats looked down at Prince with wide, frightened eyes. He called them down and the cats gathered on the countertop. Ava said they saw the coyote, through the kitchen window. Even though they'd witnessed it trotting back over the bridge they'd been too afraid to leave their hiding spots. Prince told them that that was a wise decision and also complimented them both for finding such safe spots. His wasn't nearly as safe, the shelving wasn't very sturdy. If the coyote had decided to enter the house it may have been able to jump up and knock down the shelves, sending Prince flying.

Now they had to decide what to do next. The coyote had come from, and gone back in, the direction they needed to go. How could they chance crossing over the bridge? They thought about staying put but did they really want to be here come nightfall? The coyotes would know where they were, what if more then one returned, braver with numbers, and entered the house? After a while the cats decided they couldn't stay here, they had to leave, and leave well before dark. The cats desperately wanted to make it back to the big safe house but couldn't take the direct route and go back over the bridge. They needed to find an alternate route.

They decided to keep going in the direction they had been. The looping road, they knew, would take them to some houses on the other side of the creek from Sasha and Ava's forever home. They'd have to cross the creek, much to Prince's dismay, and work their way back around, past their forever home, and eventually to the safety of the new home.

It would be a long and arduous journey and they'd have to be patient and take it slow, stopping often to look for predator signs. They could really use some bird help at this time but they hadn't seen Clarence in a few days. The eggs had hatched and he was quite busy.

Prince jumped down from the counter, telling the other cats to wait, he was going to take a look through some of the windows and see what was going on outside. He made his way out of the kitchen and went up to a big window in the front of the house. He carefully poked his head above the sill and had a clear view of the bridge, there were no coyotes in sight.

And so the cats began another journey. They left though the open basement window and slowly crept from house to house, doing their very best to stay concealed. Eventually they made it to the houses they were looking for, the ones on the other side of the creek from the old forever home. Creeping between a couple of these houses the cats soon found themselves peering at long, sloping backyards that went down towards the creek bank. They proceeded cautiously towards the creek but when there was no more cover, other then the tall grass, they began to trot quickly towards the little stream.

From behind they heard two howls, a couple of coyotes had spotted them and, just as quick as you can say shit on a stick, were giving chase. The cats ran for their lives. They had a good head start but had no plan, they were just running. They made the creek, flew down the bank and sprang nearly over the water, landing in the shallows on the other side. Quickly they flew up the opposite bank, leaving trees behind they bolted along the old familiar fence row. They ran through the field that used to be a neighbors yard, heard the coyotes coming strong, but not yet at the creek. As they ran, heads bobbing occasionally above the tall grass, Ava and Sasha caught sight of their old forever home off in the distance. It was no time to reminisce.

They'd left some trees behind, they could have climbed to safety, but Prince had cajoled them to keep going. They didn't want to be stuck in trees, with patient coyotes waiting beneath them. They heard the coyotes splashing through the water of the shallow stream and then crashing through the underbrush at the top of the bank, quickly gaining on the cats.

It didn't look good, they'd never make it to the old forever house. Sadness, despair were catching them as fast as the coyotes, so close to home, yet so far. Far from hiding places, far from the home that had once been, both in space and time.

Prince screamed at the other two cats, telling them to keep going, make for the tree, make for the tree. There was a big pine tree in the side yard of their forever home, they might make this. Suddenly Prince broke off, again screaming for the cats to keep going, to make for the tree. He screamed again, scaring them forward as he turned south heading toward his forever home, the old farm.

It was hopeless for Prince. If one or both coyotes went after him then he had no chance. He'd turned into nothing, nothing but overgrown yard and field, road and dirt, nowhere to hide. He ran forward, that's all he could do. He hoped that with his life, he could save his friends.

The coyotes, however, continued on, both intent on Sasha and Ava. They never flickered in their resolve, barely giving Prince and the path he'd taken a second glance. Prince, reaching the main road that separated the farm from the other cats' forever home, turned and screamed at the coyotes. It was no use, they were focused on the other two, but his loud screeches had caused them to pause slightly.

He watched, helpless, as the terrible carnivores closed in on his friends. They were so close, Sasha, then Ava, sprang for the tree. Sasha was in, a coyote's jaws snapped on Ava's tail, but all was not lost. The bite was too hard, severing the last few inches of her tail, as she jumped into the thick branches of the tall spruce tree and quickly scrambled to safety. Prince saw all this and was overjoyed to see that his friends had made it to safety.

The coyote with her tail came under the tree, looked up and met her eyes. It chewed slowly and swallowed, saying nothing, saying everything. Then both coyotes began to jump up into the tree. It was thick with low branches and they both came up after the cats. The cats went higher. For the coyotes this was nothing more than show, they only managed to get a few feet off the ground before crashing through bough and branches, back down to earth.

For quite some time they jumped and howled, biting at branches and cursing the cats. Two more coyotes, hearing the commotion, came to investigate. Now there were four, they settled down and began pacing at the base of the tree. One of them, appearing to be the leader, eventually looked up at the cats and gravely informed them that they'd not be leaving this tree, one or more of his friends would always be here, until the cats finally dropped, too hungry, thirsty, or tired to stave off their fall, falling into their waiting jaws. The leader went on to say that it was hopeless, didn't the cats see that? Better to give up the game now, why suffer? They'd make it quick, painless. The cats, terrified, said nothing, only staring back at their tormentors.

Sasha had been so scared that she'd peed as she jumped into the branches, she could only imagine what her friend was feeling. She made her way over to Ava and found her in shock, ignoring her injured tail and staring at the menace below. She helped Ava refocus, talking softly and encouragingly to her, then helped her groom her tail. Soon the bleeding stopped. Ava cried softly from the pain. In the distance they could hear Prince's mournful wails.

After a time some bird friends, including Clarence, heard all the noise and came to investigate. However, there was nothing they could do. Clarence lit in the tree above the cats and spoke with them, offering comfort and encouragement. The birds, along with Prince, tried their best to get the coyotes to leave but it was no use. Eventually one of the coyotes headed off to deal with Prince and he had to beat a hasty retreat to the old farm, finding a hiding place high up in one of the bigger barns. There was an opening facing north and he was able to see the predicament the other cats were in.

Mr Squirrell, whom the cats hadn't see since the fall, also gave it a try, performing the same taunting exercise that had worked well with the dog pack so long ago. The coyotes weren't falling for it, hardly even looking at the squirrel. He sadly wished the cats luck and went on his way.

The rest of the afternoon crept slowly by, it was hours before night would fall. Coyotes came and went but true to their word, they never left the tree unguarded. Prince kept hoping the dog pack would show up to rescue his friends but with four coyotes, would even TW be able to run them off? He doubted it.

Night had fallen and the coyotes didn't waver, committed it seemed. As night went on the darkness waned. The sky was cloudless and a near full moon had risen. For nocturnal eyes it was near enough to daylight to see unobscured. There would be no hope of sneaking off tonight. The cats were stuck. And it was getting cold, nothing like the winter, but with the thick fur gone the cats were soon chilled. Ava, in her weakened state, began to shiver and chatter her teeth.

Prince decided he had to do something. He knew in what general direction the dog den was. He would sneak off and try to find the dogs and implore them to help. He jumped down out of his lofty hiding place and made his way towards the door. As he approached a coyote appeared there, silhouetted eerily by the moonlight. It dashed after him, he only narrowly escaped its snapping jaws. He quickly climbed back up to his safe perch. Apparently he was being guarded too. He looked back across the road, barely able to make out the dark shadows of his friends, high up in the big pine tree. Dejectedly he put his head down on his front paws and held vigil for his friends.

Eventually, after what seemed like an eternity, the dawn began to break. With the arrival of the day all but one of the coyotes slunk off into the gathering light. The one that stayed behind kept a close eye on the cats, not appearing tired at all. Sasha crept carefully over to Ava's precarious perch. Sasha had been trying to coax her to climb to a more stable area in the tree, but Ava wasn't moving. She wasn't talking either. She had wobbled dangerously a couple times during the night, Sasha was getting worried for her sister.

The warming of the day brought some relief to the stranded cats. Ava stopped shaking and chattering, she even moved a little, inching closer to the trunk of the tree. Not a very stable spot but better than where she had been. She still wasn't talking however, and Sasha remained worried that she was in shock.

As the day progressed the cats were becoming hungry and thirsty. Ava, continuing her silence, didn't complain, although Sasha knew she was suffering. Sasha was able to find a little moisture, licking at the needles that had gathered a small amount of morning due. She was unable to get Ava to copy her behavior.

Birds came and went. Once Clarence brought a worm. He held it up to Ava's nose but she only stared blankly. Trying to push it towards her mouth Ava had turned her head and the worm dropped to the ground, Sasha watching after it longingly. The squirrel came and tried its tricks again, the one guarding coyote watched it uninterestedly.

After morning gave way to afternoon and midday approached the one coyote was replaced with two others. These two were more vocal and heckled the cats. Ava didn't even look down and appeared so unaffected by the sounds that the coyotes soon gave up and settled in under the tree.

It was a long, long day, finally giving way to a brilliant orange sunset. Sasha watched and tried to enjoy the dazzling colors. Ava had put her head down on her paws and was weaving slightly back and forth. Sasha was becoming very worried. There was some cloud cover so hopefully it wouldn't be as cold tonight but Sasha didn't think it would matter. She doubted her sister would keep her perch through another long night, she was looking more and more out of it with every hour that passed. Many times Sasha tried to get Ava to move, or at least speak. Each time she was met with only silence and the same blank stare, at least when Ava would bother looking in her direction at all.

Prince had finally slept and had been so exhausted he nearly slept the day away. He'd tried to go for help but, once again, was met by a waiting coyote, only narrowly escaping. He felt so bad and so helpless, he didn't even bother to hunt. He watched the same sunset, his growing hunger a distant pain compared the pain he felt watching his poor, trapped, friends suffer.

That night Sasha perched as close as she could to Ava, nudging her whenever she wobbled too much, helping her maintain her balance. It seemed so hopeless, but, tired, hungry, thirsty as she was, she had to keep trying. Sasha did not want to lose her friend.

In the middle of the night all four of the coyotes had joined in the watch. They were active, pacing and looking up at the cats. They sensed the inevitable, the tiger cat would soon fall and they would tear it to pieces. They were right.

Ava wobbled too far away from Sasha. She tried desperately to grab for her friend but she fell off her perch into the darkness below. The coyotes howled and jumped to meet their prey. Ava struck a firm branch hard. This seemed to jar her slightly back to her senses and she dug in her claws only just in time. The coyotes were in a frenzy, jumping and snapping at the cat, coming so close Ava could feel warm coyote breath on her fuzzy little face.

Ava looked about, her shock replaced by the reality of this situation. The time in the tree, it seemed as if it were nothing more than a foggy dream, but she was aware now. The pain from crashing into the branch snapped her out of her daze and she saw the coyotes jumping and snapping at her. She couldn't move, the branch curved down towards the trunk, closer to her enemies. And in the other direction became too thin to support her. Any movement brought her closer to the ground, closer to those snapping jaws. She looked up and saw her friend inching down to meet her. Their eyes met and Ava gave a sad mew. Sasha implored her not to give up, she was on her way, but Ava seemed to be sinking back into herself again. It seemed so hopeless, the coyotes were grabbing at her branch, they were getting closer and closer. Again she started to slip away, her eyes fluttering. She put her head back down on her paws and slowly closed her eyes, once again beginning to sway.

The cold, noises, the smells of the pine tree, they all began to recede, Ava was letting go of her surroundings. She imagined herself in the lap of her little girl, instead of precariously perched on a branch with nothing but sharp teeth below. She even began to softly purr. Sasha was horror struck as she watched her friend resigning herself to her fate. Ava swayed gently back and forth.

Ava purred as she felt the little girl's gentle hands scratch behind her ears, she was at home, at peace. A bright light was beginning to fill her eyes. The house was warm and all the lights were on, her people were with her, whispering to her, telling her how much she was loved. Finally, she was home.

The lights got brighter. She swayed, she felt herself tumble from the warm lap. Into nothingness she fell.

There was a loud screech, heart wrenching, ear splitting, follow by a louder blast like a horn. A horn? Ava hit the ground. There were many noises that she did not recognize. The lights were still very bright, she kept her eyes firmly shut. She heard growls and shouts. There were sounds that seemed to come from a distant past. She didn't know where she was or what was happening around her. The ground was cold, she'd been in a tree, she'd fallen. Ava opened her eyes.

A man had emerged from a vehicle that had slid to a stop only a few yards away, its bright headlights illuminating the tree. A truck? What was this? Ava could not wrap her head around what was going on. The vehicle's horn blasted again and again. The coyotes had turned to confront this unforeseen threat, just as Ava had lost her balance. They were shocked, but angry, and did not immediately retreat. They would have, last year, but they hadn't seen man in so long.

The first man out of the truck, in what looked like a smooth and well practiced motion, quickly pointed his hand at the tree. Almost instantly fire and painfully loud noise exploded from his hand. In almost the same instant Ava was sprayed by a warm liquid and chunks of undefined matter, a coyote dropped dead right beside her, its head a bloody mess. The situation finally registered and the others fled, followed closely by more fire and thunder.

There were two men, they had flashlights and approached the tree. Ava recognized the first, by sight and smell, it was one of her people, she sat on the ground and, amazingly, continued to purr. The man found her there. He spoke gently to her, he seemed amazed in his own way, and he reached out to stroke her fur.

Sasha remained in the middle of the tree, too shocked to move, still frighted from all the noise. She eyed the dead coyote warily. Soon she was discovered by the men. It took a long time but eventually she calmed down and allowed herself to be coaxed out of the tree. She was embraced by the man and looked up at him, big blue eyes filling with tears as beautiful memories flooded her little mind.

The cats were brought into the cab of the truck. Water was poured into a built in cup holder between the front seats and they drank. The water did Ava a world of good and she was soon regaining her senses. The cats were safely shut in the truck while the men went into the old forever home. They wondered, for a short time, if they would soon be joining them back home, together at last.

It wasn't long and the men re-appeared, carrying a few small items the cats didn't recognize as anything significant. The men got back in the truck, and after spending a short time soothing the cats and giving them some jerked meat to chew on, they started the truck and drove away. As they left the neighborhood the cats both noticed two shining bright possum eyes staring at them from the neighbor's house with the branch through the window, the first house they'd entered after their people had gone. Such a long time ago. They smiled and waved. The possum, who now called that house his home, quickly wondered if he'd be able to do that much longer, smiled and waved back.

It was a long trip and they stopped only once. The men had got out, relieved themselves, and dumped the contents of red cans stored in the pickup's bed into a opening on the side. Then they were off again. They were happy to once again be in the company of their people but felt bad for leaving all of their friends behind so suddenly. They hadn't even gotten a chance to say goodbye. They especially felt bad about Prince, they had no idea if he had made it to safety. For a short time they had tried to convey to the men that they needed to go back for Prince, but the humans just took this as a ploy for attention. They talked soothingly to the cats and stroked their fur, so the cats settled down realizing there was nothing they could do for their friends but wish them good fortune.

Eventually they arrived at their destination. It was a compound with many people and a large imposing fence. Here and there, at the top of fence posts, were stuck gory things. The cats did not concern themselves with this.

Other men opened the gate and the truck drove in. The cats immediately recognized the little girl as she came running from the house, glad to see her dad returning.

While she was giving him a great big hug her dad told her he had a surprise for her. Breaking the embrace he led her around to the cab of the truck. She looked inside and her mouth dropped open. Tears began to gush from her eyes and stream down her cheeks and she seemed unable to move or speak. Sasha strolled forward on the seat and looked at her, then mewed quietly. This broke the little girl's trance and she rushed forward, giving her cats a long missed loving embrace.

The End

Epilogue:

Prince witnessed the reunion and was overjoyed to see his friends rescued, but he could not go join them, the coyotes had run his way. He didn't dare leave his safe perch.

A overwhelming mixture of joy and sadness flowed through him as he watched the truck rumble out of sight.

He'd wanted to run to them but had been too afraid. After a time he found that the coyotes were long gone, the gunfire had sent them scurrying back to the woods. He despaired at his hesitation, maybe he could have joined them, but he'd never know for sure.

Later he would meet up with the dog pack and share the story. There would be many tears, especially from Slow, who felt great joy at hearing a story with a happy ending. The dogs also took it as a sign that maybe their own people would soon return. They rejoiced at the thought.

Prince said goodbye to the dogs and hoped they would visit again but as he turned to leave, the dogs told Prince that he should stay with them.

The dogs pleaded with Prince, giving him many reasons to stay. The gray cat that lived with the dogs could really use some cat company. That, and it would be easier to protect Prince from coyotes, which never got near the Den. Prince finally relented and off he went, reasonably happy for a former pet now living off the land.

Made in the USA
Lexington, KY
18 July 2018